Improvisation

By the Author

Harmony

Worth the Risk

Sea Glass Inn

Improvisation

Improvisation

by

Karis Walsh

2013

IMPROVISATION

ISBN 10: 1-60282-872-5
ISBN 13: 978-1-60282-872-8

This Trade Paperback Original Is Published By
Bold Strokes Books, Inc.
P.O. Box 249
Valley Falls, NY 12185

First Edition: May 2013

Credits
Editor: Ruth Sternglantz
Production Design: Susan Ramundo
Cover Design By Sheri (graphicartist2020@hotmail.com)

Acknowledgments

Revisiting the world I created in *Harmony* and reconnecting with some favorite characters has been a wonderful experience. I've come out of the process filled with gratitude for every reader who has taken a chance and bought one of my books. For every person who has contacted me through e-mail or Facebook or my blogs. For every romance fan I've had the privilege of meeting in person at a book signing or other event.

Whether you've read all my novels or are just joining me now, with *Improvisation*, this book is for you. Thank you for taking the time to travel with me through the world of my imagination. Enjoy!

Dedication

For Cindy
With all my love and all my heart

CHAPTER ONE

Tina Nelson's fingers played a cascading waterfall of notes, echoed moments later by Andrea Taylor's viola, while her mind raced several measures ahead. She was sure Andy had practiced diligently before this session, but Tina hadn't even glanced at the music since the last time they had played it together, over six months ago. The rehearsal was a casual one between two friends as they worked the kinks out of a duet they'd played before, but Andy had obviously prepared for it. When Tina had arrived at Andy's—fifteen minutes late, after frantically searching for the right piece among the numerous piles of sheet music scattered throughout her apartment—Andy had already set up two chairs and had written out an agenda for the session. Luckily, Tina enjoyed the rush of being a few steps behind and fighting to catch up. She noticed some tricky string changes coming, and she shifted her hand up the violin's neck into fifth position to handle the difficult passage more easily.

"Stop doing that," Andy said, continuing to play without missing a beat when Tina morphed the Mozart into an old fiddle tune.

Tina sighed and returned to the music in front of her. Mozart's second string duo was one of her favorites—fiery and demanding and passionate. Perfectly suited to her and Andy's style of playing. But, today, the stems on the notes resembled prison bars, and she felt too restless to stay within their confines. She tried to behave for half a page before a series of notes led her back to the familiar fiddle song.

This time, she managed to pull Andy along with her for a few bars. "Incorrigible," Andy said as she stopped playing and balanced her bow on her lap.

"Irresistible," Tina offered instead. She considered it a personal triumph every time she was able to tempt Andy off the transcribed path of perfection.

Andy penciled in a note on her music. "Now, every time I play this section, I'll want to switch songs," she said, a small smile belying her cranky tone. She took out a yellow highlighter and emphatically colored her notation.

"What did you write?" Tina asked, leaning over to peek at Andy's music. Notes filled the margins, color-coded for her convenience. "Do not have fun?"

Brooke Stanton tapped on the door of Andy's music room, the spare bedroom in their apartment. "Are you taking a break?"

"Just long enough to get Tina back in line," Andy said.

"Could be hours," Tina added, watching her friend's small grin turn into a bright smile as Brooke walked into the room. She swiped two of Andy's colored pens while her attention was diverted. Tina had slept with plenty of women she met at the weddings where she played with Andy and the two other members of their string quartet, but those relationships rarely lasted beyond the next weekend's gig. Andy had only slept with one—for once straying from her orderly behavior and dramatically choosing the bride instead of a bridesmaid—but the relationship had lasted almost two years so far. Everyone who knew Andy and Brooke expected those two years to stretch into forever.

"Was that Mozart?" Brooke asked, stepping farther into the room and resting her hands on Andy's shoulders.

"It was 'Little Brown Jug,'" Andy said. "But it was *supposed* to be Mozart."

"Poor sweetheart, is Tina driving you crazy?" Brooke winked at Tina before leaning down to kiss Andy on the cheek. Tina winked back. She and Brooke were often coconspirators in their attempts to bring out Andy's more playful side. Tina watched Andy turn her face to meet Brooke's kiss. It was simple and quick, but the love behind it was difficult to miss. Tina smiled, glad to see her friend's happiness. Brooke was the kind of woman who might even have made Tina give up her routine seduction of bridesmaids. Thank God, Andy had found her first.

"I'll let the two of you get back to work," Brooke said as she straightened up. "Andy, I bought a can of tomatoes when we were at that Italian grocery downtown, but I can't seem to find it."

"Second shelf, behind the soup," Andy said as she shuffled through her music.

"Because *t* comes after *s*?" Tina asked.

"That's just how I put them away," Andy said, sounding indignant. "I don't alphabetize my canned goods."

"Anymore," Brooke called from the kitchen.

Andy's cheeks turned slightly pink, but she pretended to ignore the comment even though she couldn't hide her smile as she clearly enjoyed Brooke's teasing. "Let's practice the third movement. Without any fiddle tunes this time."

Tina's laugh changed to a sigh. Back to work.

❖

An hour later, Tina shoved her sheet music haphazardly into her bag. After two more unsuccessful attempts to sway Andy away from the written notes, Tina had given up and concentrated on the Mozart. Even she felt satisfied with the final play-through. She and Andy handled the challenging timing easily, coordinating the two intricate parts with a comfort developed over years of playing together.

Boring old practice had a predictable but limited outcome—improvement. Tina preferred to improvise because she never knew what the result would be. Unpredictable, with limitless possibilities. But even though an impromptu fiddle jam session would have been more exciting, Tina knew she'd appreciate Andy's insistence on perfection when they played the piece in front of an audience. The chamber music festival would be her last performance with Andy for at least three months because Tina had stupidly promised to work with her cousin in Spokane. Temporarily. She shifted restlessly in her seat, tired of sitting still for so long. She didn't relish the prospect of spending so much time far from her friends and too close to her family.

"I'll miss this," Andy echoed Tina's thoughts.

"Me too," Tina said. She toyed with a tuning peg on her violin, tightening the A string. She plucked it. Sharp. She returned it to its original tension and laid the violin in its velvet-lined case. "But Spokane in the spring…they write songs about that, don't they?"

"They should," Andy said with a smile. "All the cows are blooming."

"And the tumbleweeds aren't yet dry enough to tumble."

"It's a beautiful city," Brooke said from the doorway. "Rivers and lakes and parks. A brilliant cultural scene. Tons of great restaurants…"

"Thank you, Spokane Board of Tourism," Tina said as she followed Brooke into the living room. The coffee table was set with food for Brooke and Andy, and a plate of pasta and glass of wine sat on a tray next to the chair Tina always used. Brooke had simply expected her to stay for dinner—a sure sign Tina was spending too much time in their apartment. Intruding on their privacy. And neglecting her own romantic life. "Do you have any brochures?"

"Even better," Brooke said as she sat on the couch and folded her legs underneath her. "I happen to know a beautiful woman who, I'll bet, would be willing to act as your personal tour guide."

Tina groaned. She had walked right into Brooke's trap. She took a bite of garlicky, spicy penne before she answered. "I appreciate it, but I'm sure I'll be too busy to socialize."

Andy laughed and choked on her pasta. "When have you *ever* been too busy to womanize? Sorry, I meant *socialize*."

"Funny," Tina said. "But I have to design Peter's website and help him create a marketing plan and—"

Brooke waved her fork in the air. "You've managed to have other plans every time Jan's come to Seattle. I'll bet you can find an hour or two over the next three months to meet her for a drink."

Tina balanced her plate on her lap and took a sip of wine. Brooke was partially right—Tina was going to need plenty to drink and plenty of female companionship to get her through the uncomfortable reunion with her family. And she certainly wouldn't disagree with Brooke's description of her friend as beautiful. Tina hadn't had a chance to talk to Jan Carroll at Brooke's wedding rehearsal, but she had been very aware of her, sitting alone in the back of the church. A fraction of her mind had concentrated on playing the familiar quartet music, but most of it had been pleasantly occupied with the imagined sight of Jan's dark blond hair released from those barrettes, reflecting gold as it fell around her shoulders. The feel of Jan's skin as Tina stripped off her silk pantsuit and slipped her hands around that slender waist…Tina would have had Jan's phone number before the bride and groom made it down the aisle if it had been one of the group's normal wedding gigs. But she had needed to stay with Andy, who was distraught because she thought she had lost Brooke. Then Brooke had fallen in love with Andy and turned into a matchmaker, and Jan was now off-limits for Tina. Tina wanted nothing more serious than an affair or three in Spokane, but she suspected Brooke was busily planning a double wedding.

"I'll try to make time, but no promises. Besides, I'm not looking for anything serious right now. Or ever, right, Andy?"

"Jan's great, Tina," Andy said in a serious voice. "You'll like her, and it'll be good for you to have a friend over there. Someone to get you away from your family now and then."

Traitor. Andy was no help. She had joined the "serious relationship" cult and apparently was willing to help Brooke in her recruiting efforts. Even now, she stared at Brooke as if Stradivari himself had carved her curves out of a rare piece of wood. Tina was thrilled to see her so…content. Andy had always been wound a bit tight, and Brooke had managed to loosen her up, get her back in tune. But Tina wasn't Andy. An occasional casual affair for stress release was all the retuning she needed. She finished the last of her wine and set the glass down a little harder than she meant to.

Brooke poured more wine in Tina's glass. "What's the situation with you and your family? Or shouldn't I ask?"

Tina had been hoping for a change in subject, but talking about her family was as bad as being pushed into Jan's arms. She swirled the wine and watched the light play off the ruby liquid.

"We're just distant, I guess. When Dad was alive, we'd go visit a couple times a year. Grandmother would criticize my mom for everything—how she was raising me without enough discipline, what a little hellion I was. Dad would try to defend me and Mom, to make everyone get along, but the visits were always a mess." Tina paused and took a drink of the rich and fruity wine. Her dad had kept up his efforts to bring the family together until he died, when Tina was eight. Then the trips to Spokane had stopped. Tina's grandmother hadn't had a chance to know her during junior high and high school, when her mom had been sick and she had grown up faster than most teenagers.

Now she'd get to know the adult Tina, the grown-up hellion. Tina smiled at the thought.

"To families," Andy said as she raised her glass in a mock salute. "Where would alcohol sales be without them?"

Tina returned the gesture and watched Brooke curl closer to Andy on the couch. Her friend had been forced to be an adult at an early age as well. But maturity sat easily on her, and she seemed to crave the security and stability of her relationship. Tina had shrugged off the weight of responsibility after her mother had died, and she had no intention of finding someone else to depend on her. She had experienced love and loss. She didn't plan to go through it again.

"So what about this cousin?" Brooke asked. "You've agreed to help him, so he can't be all bad."

"He's okay," Tina said with a shrug. "We played together when we were kids and he's kept in touch. Letters or e-mails on holidays, that sort of thing." She laughed shortly at the memory of their latest awkward exchange. "Somewhere along the way, our conversations became little more than weather reports, and the most personal answer either of us gives to the question *How are you?* is the local temperature. It's easier for him, since there are actual seasons in Spokane. But how many ways can I say *It's rainy with occasional sunbreaks*?"

"Maybe he's desperate to keep any sort of relationship going," Brooke said, her voice soft. "*It's unseasonably warm this spring* might mean *I want to talk to you, but I don't know how to get past this rift*."

Tina shook her head. Peter probably only wrote to her because he felt guilty after his side of the family abandoned her. And she only answered, year after year, because she didn't want to be rude. She had more feelings for the weather girl on the local news. "Nice idea, Brooke, but the truth is, we feel some stupid family obligation to keep writing, but we don't care enough to get beyond the most stereotypically superficial of topics. I'm going to help him because Dad would've wanted me to, but after this trip, we can stop the meaningless chit-chat. It'll be a relief for both of us, I'm sure."

"Cloudy, with a noticeable chill in the air," Andy said, without looking up from her dinner.

Tina ignored her comment. She would accept the uncomfortable obligations to family and to Brooke, but after this trip, she would be free of them. No more Peter. And definitely no more Jan.

CHAPTER TWO

Jan ended the call and dropped the phone into the pocket of her blazer. Her third-period class was already filing into the room, so she controlled her desire to drop her head onto the desk and cry. Instead, she silently recited the students' names as they sat down, in an effort to reorient herself. Sophomore Geometry. Twenty-one students. Lesson number twelve. She watched them chat and laugh as they pulled out notebooks and rulers while she wondered if she'd be able to get through the hour without needing to ask one of them what she was supposed to be teaching.

The doctor's words took up all the space in her mind, pushing away the theorems and proofs from today's lesson plan. She had been expecting a call about her dad's injured shoulder, not about the warning signs the doctor had noticed while examining him. *Possibility of early onset Alzheimer's. We'll run more tests. Has your father shown any of these symptoms?* No, but she seemed to be experiencing all of them right now. Her dad's fall and subsequent stay in the hospital had left her scared and worried. Planning to move him into her partially renovated house and arranging for a nurse while she was at school had left her frantic and harried. But the doctor's news had left her numb. Empty. Lost.

She registered that the students were watching her silently, waiting for her to start class. The bell must have rung, somewhere in the distance outside of her new reality. She stood and began to teach as if programmed. The rhythm of the class was familiar, and she could follow her carefully organized and structured lesson plans in her sleep. Which was lucky, because she felt as responsive and alive as a zombie. Step one, review last week's assignments to make sure the base for this week's skills was solid. If the foundation was weak, it wouldn't support the weight of new information. In class, as in life. She had finally started to build a life here in Spokane after years of living like a nomad. But that plan had always included both her and her dad, with their relationship and memories intact. Without her only family, her foundation was nothing but empty space.

Jan shook off the panic threatening to overwhelm her and walked to the whiteboard, where she sketched several quadrilaterals. She felt a slight easing of tension as she drew each one. The comforting shapes and angles and lines made sense. The lengths and widths and heights were constant and always offered the correct answer if manipulated properly. Simple. Logical.

Jan reviewed the old material and answered a few questions before she collected homework and turned to new business. She usually loved teaching this section—another one of her preemptive strikes against the age-old *When will I ever use this?* math question—and she struggled against her mental fog. Her students needed her to be engaged and present. Tonight, when she was away from her obligations and the structured script of her lesson, she would fall apart. But not now.

She passed out sheets of heavy drawing paper and soft pencils. "This week, we'll be examining the link between geometry and art. Later on, we'll study some actual paintings, but today, I want you to be the artists." She paused for the expected groans from the teenagers. "Don't worry, you aren't being graded on skill, just participation. I want you to draw a sketch of me, full-length, standing next to my desk. Just try to make an accurate drawing, and don't use this as a way to get revenge on me for last week's pop quiz."

She stood in the front of the classroom, with one hand resting on her desk. The lesson had the benefit and challenge of frequent breaks while the students worked, and she needed to use those moments to recharge and refocus, not to dwell on the uncertain future. So she tried to stay still while her class squinted first at her and then at their drawings, erasing and redrawing almost every line.

"Eyes on your own paper, Christine," she said.

"But his is funny," Christine said, gesturing at her boyfriend's drawing. "Your head looks *huge*."

"I'm sure Tom is just symbolically representing the size of my brain," Jan teased, taking the brief moment while the class's attention was on the couple to surreptitiously glance at her vibrating cell. Another message from her old college friend Brooke, not the doctor. The lesser of two evils. "Don't worry, we'll get a chance to see everyone's pictures once you've finished."

"You owe the jar a dollar," Alex said from his seat in the front row as she started to collect the sketches. "You checked your phone."

Jan sighed, fished out her wallet, and crammed a dollar bill into the jar on her desk while the class erupted into giggles. Apparently, she hadn't been as subtle as she had thought. She had a strict no-phones, no-texting policy in class, and the year-end pizza parties paid for with the fines were sometimes extravagant. This was the first time she had contributed, and she planned to have Brooke reimburse her for the dollar. It was, by far, the least Brooke could do, given the favor she was asking.

"We've learned how to describe shapes by giving values to their dimensions. Now, we're going to express the relationship between two shapes as a number." Jan launched into the lesson on ratio and proportion, hoping it would do double duty of getting her mind off both her dad's health and Brooke's messages about Tina's impending visit. Numbers and logic. Easily definable and orderly. They had always helped her in the past, giving her a sense of calm and structure and distance. Why not now, when she needed them most?

"What are some ways we can compare two people mathematically?" Jan listed the students' suggestions on the whiteboard. Height, weight, strength, GPA. "Excellent. And what are some comparisons that can't be expressed as a ratio?"

Beauty, popularity, kindness. Jan wrote the list of nonquantifiable traits. Vague and indefinite. Her mind half on the class discussion, Jan let the recollection of Tina Nelson occupy a small part of her thoughts. Tina had a classic beauty that could be measured by a scientist. Proportions, height, angles. All symmetrical and pleasing, but the addition of indefinable qualities of confidence and sensuality made her truly charismatic. Tina had been scoping out the bridesmaids while she played the violin at Brooke's wedding rehearsal, and then her attention had turned to Jan. She had been sitting in the back row of the church, wanting to support Brooke while keeping out of the way of her judgmental family. Unobtrusive. But Tina had found her. Jan recognized a player when she saw one, when she felt the almost physical force of one's interest. And, two years ago, when Jan thought she'd finally had her life on the right track, she had been prepared to have a weekend fling. To let Tina seduce her.

Jan didn't want to let her thoughts go down that path again. She had lived the seduction in her imagination too many times. Two years ago, she had everything under control. She wanted to settle in Spokane, make it a permanent home after a childhood spent moving from one air force base to another. She had a job, and her newly retired military father seemed content to make the apartment they'd rented when he was stationed at Fairchild into his permanent home. Next on Jan's list was a home of her own, and then she would start the search for a partner, someone to share her new life. But in the meantime, an out-of-town affair with Tina was too appealing to refuse. A little fun before Jan went back to building her life in Spokane. But Brooke's decision to cancel the wedding had meant a change in plans for Jan, as well.

Ancient history. Jan turned her attention back to geometry and to the student sketches she had pinned on the wall. She pointed out flaws in the proportions of her body parts. Usually, she had to keep her vanity in check when some of the students' drawings seemed to caricature her least-desirable features, but today it seemed as if the students had managed to capture the disjointed way she felt inside. Out of whack. In Tom's drawing, her head was much too big for her body, and it felt the same in reality, so swollen with thoughts and worries she thought it might explode. And she was certain she'd be lurching through the rest of her day, as if walking on the imbalanced and uneven limbs her students had drawn.

She finally broke the class into small groups and set them to work measuring and averaging the ratios between hand and arm length, arm span and height. Breaking complex human beings into a series of numbers, while she returned to the uncomfortable issue of Tina's visit. Would she be able to resist the temptation of a brief affair? A little fun in the midst of chaos? She had to. Having Tina flow in and out of her life had been an acceptable idea when Jan had been on track to accomplish her goals. But her plans were derailed, and now a fling would only be a reminder of the elusive stability she had to put off for an indefinite amount of time. Life on military bases had made it difficult to maintain friendships, and Brooke was one of the few constants in Jan's life. She had been a best friend and confidante, always dependable and present even when they were in separate cities. Jan couldn't be anything less for Brooke. Jan would play the polite host and show Tina her city, but she would do whatever it took to keep a safe distance between them.

"For tonight's homework, I want you to measure as many people as you can and find the average ratios. Just be sure to ask for their permission before you start measuring body parts," Jan said with a smile as she wrapped up the lesson just before the bell. She let the students' laughter die down before continuing. "Use those numbers when you draw *another* picture of me by my desk, and tomorrow we'll compare the two."

The students filed out, their voices and laughter increasing in volume as soon as they were released from the confines of the classroom. Jan shut the door, blocking out the noise from the hallway. She paced behind her desk. She had been waiting for the chance to be alone, but now the room seemed too empty. Too quiet. As soon as the halls cleared, she went to the teachers' break room and poured a cup of coffee. She picked one of the square tables, comforting with its right angles and even sides, and stared out the window while she stirred several packets of raw sugar into the strong coffee. The hawthorn trees were just starting to show rosy blooms. Spring. Just last week she had been thrilled by the millions of tiny signs of summer approaching. She had saved and planned and organized so the summer could be devoted to renovating and decorating her house. Now all she saw before her was a series of visits to the doctor, of tests and evaluations, of bad news.

"Are you okay?" Chloe Porter stood close to her chair. Jan hadn't even heard her approach.

"I'm fine," Jan said, not meaning it at all. She gestured at the seat across from her. "Join me?"

Chloe sat down and toyed with the string of her tea bag. "How's your dad doing?"

"He's fine," Jan said, unable to stop before she repeated the vague and untrue adjective. Chloe had been friendly toward her since Jan had started teaching at Spokane Heights. She'd been slow to warm up to Chloe, reluctant to get too close, as she fought her ingrained tendency to see every relationship or home as transient. Maybe she had been right to keep their friendship superficial since she didn't have any idea what changes the next year would bring.

"Good," Chloe said, her voice neutral. She dunked her tea bag several times. "You know, if you ever need…If there's anything I can do to help…"

"Thanks, but I'm…okay," Jan said. She neatly folded the empty sugar packets and set them next to her coffee mug. Family problems were too personal to share. But *Tina* wasn't a family problem. Asking for a favor to help get through the ordeal of meeting with her seemed acceptable. "Actually, I could use some help. A friend of a friend is coming to town, and I promised to take her out for drinks and show her around. I'd appreciate having some company so I don't have to be alone with her."

"Of course I'll go," Chloe said with a smile. Jan felt a stab of guilt because she kept pushing Chloe's friendship away, only letting her close now when she needed a favor. Jan had been focused on protecting herself. It hadn't occurred to her that Chloe might be lonely, too. "So what's wrong with her?"

"Nothing at all," Jan said, surprised by her immediate and unequivocal response. She forced her voice to stay casual. "I've only seen her playing violin with her string quartet. We haven't met, and I just thought I'd be more comfortable if we made it more of a group outing."

"And not a date?" Chloe asked in a teasing tone. "You're blushing, so I'm guessing she's not bad looking."

Jan laughed. Her mind was preoccupied with worry, but her body still managed to betray her awareness of Tina's good looks. She moved in her chair as if squirming away from the imagined feel of Tina's hands stroking her arms and brushing through her hair. "She's gorgeous, but definitely a playgirl. My friend Brooke has made it her mission to set us up, but I'm not looking for a casual fling right now. To be perfectly honest, I could use a safety net to keep me from falling for her because the landing would be way too painful."

"Ah, I see. The fair damsel wants someone to protect her from Don Juan. Say no more, I'll be a strict chaperone. It'll give me some good practice before this year's prom. Although, if you really want someone to take her off your hands—so to speak—you might be better off asking Sasha."

An image of Tina and the history teacher together flashed through Jan's mind. They'd complement each other well. Tina had the sleek and fast look of an expensive sports car while Sasha had all the right curves. Both out for a good time, and both gay. Jan decided not to look too closely at her decision to stick with straight Chloe.

"The three of us will be fine. I just need you there as a buffer. I want to show her a little of the city, not get her laid," Jan said, attributing her wistful-sounding voice to stress and not hormones. As long as Chloe never left them alone, she could get through a few hours with Tina and keep her virtue, and her sanity, intact.

CHAPTER THREE

The rain on the windshield of Tina's old Corolla turned to sleet once she was in the Cascades. Unseasonably heavy banks of snow lined I-90, but the pavement was bare and wet. Her hope that a freak spring snowstorm would close the pass melted away as she sped by Snoqualmie's chalets and deserted ski lifts. Half an hour later, she flicked off her wipers as she came down from the summit and into a landscape strangely and subtly different from the one she had left so recently. Long-tailed magpies, harlequin versions of the crows she was used to seeing, scavenged along the highway. Pine trees predominated over the ubiquitous firs of the western half of Washington. And she knew she would have to drive for days before she came across another city the size of Seattle.

Tina pulled off the highway in Ellensburg. She had been driving only a little over two hours on her five-hour trip, so she didn't have any way to justify a long lunch break, except by admitting that she was in no hurry to get to her destination. Reason enough to stop. She parked in the lot of a diner just off the freeway exit and climbed out of her car. The faded red roof and flaking brown paint were incongruous with the brightly painted banner proclaiming they had the best food in Ellensburg. Tina had her doubts, but she felt compelled to give the dive a shot at proving itself. A heavy wind caught her by surprise as she was rummaging through the trunk for her backpack, and she dug a rubber band out of her suitcase and tied her hair into a ponytail to keep it off her face.

She settled into a booth and scanned the menu. Typical truck-stop food, heavy and greasy. Yum. Just what she wanted. She ordered a cheeseburger and cherry malt before she brought out her sketch pad and colored pencils. The temperature outside was close to the fifty-five degrees she had left in Seattle, but the air felt drier. And the wind blowing through Snoqualmie Pass was crazy, even though she had been to Ellensburg enough times, either as a stopover on the way to the eastern side of the state or for the occasional music symposium at CWU, to be accustomed to it. She felt dusty and windblown after just the short trip from her car to the restaurant.

She quickly drew a valley she had spotted while she drove. Red-brown basalt formations and a couple of horses grazing on the sparse grass. She wasn't much of an artist without a computer program to help, and she decided her horses looked more like llamas than anything equine. Still, something about the color palette intrigued her, and she wanted to capture it on paper. Faded gold, dried sage, dirt brown. The colors of the dead of summer, even though it was spring. Everything was lush and green at home.

"What a pretty landscape," the waitress remarked, interrupting Tina's concentration. "If you want to keep working, I can set your food over here."

"No, I'm finished," Tina said as she moved her sketch pad to make room for her cheeseburger. The waitress set a metal cup with extra cherry malt next to the whipped-cream-covered fountain glass. Tina glanced at the waitress's name tag. "If you have a break soon, Theresa, I'd be happy to draw your portrait."

Theresa laughed. "Now you save that charm for someone closer to your own age, honey. Besides, after seeing how you drew those poor cows, I'm afraid to find out what you'd do to me."

Tina had a novel with her, but it sat untouched by her plate as she slowly ate her lunch, too distracted to concentrate on the story. She alternated between flirting with Theresa every time she walked by and watching a red-winged blackbird perched on a branch outside her window, his red epaulets shining brightly in the sun. She finished all too soon and didn't have any more reason to hang around. She took a last drink of her malt and wiped condensation from the metal cup off her hands before she gathered her art supplies. She left a generous tip on the table and battled the wind back to her car.

She watched the scenery with interest, at first. The designer in her loved the contrasts of lines and textures in the farmland bordering the highway. The young spring plants were too small for her to be able to tell what they were, but blue roadside signs identified fields green with potatoes, alfalfa, and wheat nestled between stretches of barren, sagebrush-dotted cow pastures. Low, curving hills were intersected by the straight lines created by humans—long irrigation pipes and perfectly spaced rows of crops. A group of white, angular windmills grew out of a hillside like a flower bed planted by huge aliens.

She exited at a rest stop to write down some of the ideas the scenery was inspiring, but all the picnic tables were protected by concrete windbreaks, and the stubby trees looked permanently windblown. She didn't want to battle the elements again, so she sat in her car and wrote a detailed plan for a website inspired by the arc of irrigation pipes and the tapered blades of the windmills. She mentally ran through her client list, but none of them was a good match for her idea. The mock-up would look great in her portfolio, though, and the project would give her another way to fill her free time in Spokane.

Even after she finished her notes, she sat in her car and just let herself sit and breathe for a few minutes. From her parking place, she could see the highway, winding west toward Ellensburg and east to the Columbia River Gorge at Vantage and on to Spokane. A few cars and semis traveled on the road, and she could see a small roadside town consisting of a hotel, market, and gas station. Still, the sense of space pervaded in spite of the scattered marks of civilization. She hadn't realized how compressed she had become until now, when she finally had room to take a deep breath. Her job as a freelance graphic designer made telecommuting fairly easy to manage, but she had still needed to take care of what felt like a million boring details to make this summer trip feasible. Add a busy season of work and wedding gigs and sleepless nights worried about revisiting her family, and she had been left with too little energy to do more than hang out in the comfort of Andy and Brooke's married-couple routine. At least in Spokane, she didn't expect to have trouble finding a stimulating nightlife, the universal antidote to small-town boredom.

Back on the road, and about an hour out of Ellensburg, the novelty of the landscape began to wear off. Tina plugged in her MP3 player and cranked up the radio's volume, tapping the steering wheel restlessly as she drove across miles of nothing much. She might have a beat-up car, but she had the highest quality speakers money could buy. She was thankful she had brought her own music along because she was certain the local programming wouldn't be her style.

For long stretches, the most interesting things to see were plastic bags and tumbleweeds caught on the barbed-wire fences lining the highway. A dilapidated house or broken-down tractor occasionally broke the monotony of her trip. How many manifestos were being penned behind those rusted front doors? The desire to be finished with the long drive warred with her reluctance to see her family again. Avoidance won a small battle, and she stopped for a latte and a chance to flirt with the barista at a Starbucks in the sadly misnamed town of Ritzville before she finally gave in and pushed over the speed limit for the last sixty miles to Spokane.

❖

As she got closer to the city, the barren landscape began to look more like home, with more trees and greener grass. Instead of the urban sprawl around Seattle, though, the outskirts of Spokane were dotted with lakes and sparse residential neighborhoods. One minute she was on an empty stretch of highway with ducks soaring over her car to settle on a roadside lake, and the next, she was right in the middle of downtown Spokane with its strangely familiar skyline. She had been away far too long to feel like she recognized the city, with its old redbrick buildings that somehow managed to dominate the taller and more modern glass structures.

Against her better judgment, Tina bypassed the exit leading to her hotel and stayed on I-90 until she reached the east edge of the city. Might as well get the family reunion over, first thing. She shuffled through the mess on her passenger seat, pushing aside music catalogs and spare fiddle strings, and found the directions Peter had sent. She felt grubby and irritable and tempted by the promise of a hot shower, a stiff drink, and some food at the hotel, but she wouldn't be able to relax until she saw her grandmother and Peter.

She drove past a mall and a series of chain restaurants. Anymall, Anytown, USA. How did her cousin's small nursery and garden shop compete with these box stores? Advertising and web design could only do so much to attract customers, and Tina hoped Peter didn't expect any miracles from her. Only a few blocks later, though, the bland familiarity of the shopping area gave way to a quieter neighborhood with older apartment buildings interspersed with boutique stores. Even with the family visit looming, Tina spotted several shops she wanted to check out while she was in town. She dug around for a pen while she was stopped at a light and scrawled the name of an Irish pub on the back of Peter's directions. There was a sign advertising live music in the window, and she had brought her fiddle in the hope of finding some place to play. She dropped the pen while she was trying to screw the cap back on and missed the turn to the nursery.

She finally made her way back to Nelson's Garden Store and let her car idle while she sat in the parking lot. She checked her reflection in the mirror on her visor. A ratty beige fisherman knit sweater, torn jeans, and no makeup. The hasty ponytail she had made in Ellensburg had done little to protect her hair from the wind, and long brown strands hung loose around her face.

"This was a mistake," she whispered, not sure if she meant skipping a stop at the hotel or the entire summer. Or both. She used her fingers to comb her hair before she slipped the rubber band on it again. She was about to put the car in reverse, come back when she felt more in control of herself and her appearance, when someone tapped on her window. Peter.

"Tina?" she heard him ask through the glass. She turned off her car and opened the door.

"Hello, Peter." She was unprepared for his smile and for the hug he gave her as soon as she got out of the car. She awkwardly gave his back a quick pat before she pulled away.

"It's great to see you. How was your drive?" He spoke quickly, barely stopping for answers, and Tina could see his nervousness as clearly as she felt her own. "Come see the shop. I'm glad to have you here to help pull us into the twenty-first century."

He laughed as if he was joking, but Tina felt pulled back in time the moment she walked through the door. "Oh wow," she said as she skirted around some bags of fertilizer stacked near the door. Racks of seeds, rows of plants, and tall piles of paving stones competed for her attention. Mundane gardening tools and gloves sat on shelves next to ornamental metal hummingbirds and bejeweled frogs. She was assaulted by a mass of smells as well, from handmade soaps and flowering plants and what had to be the fertilizer she had seen by the door. The air felt thicker inside than out, textured with floral and musty, earthy scents.

"It's kind of cluttered," Peter said. He fiddled with a display of canning supplies, wearing the expression of an indulgent and fond parent as he rearranged the Mason jars.

Tina laughed at his understatement. "I love it," she said, surprised by how much she really did. She had come prepared to hate her family and everything about them, but the cacophony of colors and smells and growing things was too irresistible. She could sell this place. "It's like an old-fashioned general store."

Peter smiled at her, and the collage of ideas fluttering through her mind dropped out of sight, as if she had lost her place in a book she was reading. She had been picturing him as the young boy she remembered from childhood, with a vague overlay of the teenager who had come to her mom's funeral and awkwardly expressed his condolences. But the man in front of her could have been her father, transported through time and back into her life. Sandy-brown hair and eyes the color of cool jade, just like Tina's own. Pale skin and features that seemed designed for serious concentration until he smiled and his whole face lit up. Just like her dad.

"Come see the greenhouses," he said, apparently not noticing her sudden shock. She followed him through humid plastic structures, making appropriate comments about the potted herbs and veggie starts while she struggled to collect and control her emotions. This was exactly why she avoided family. Everything was too complex. Never simple.

As if summoned by Tina's thoughts, her grandmother appeared in the doorway, framed by some hanging baskets dripping with fuchsias. Tina felt another jolt of recognition as she saw her father's features and build in her grandmother's form. But Francine Nelson's wrinkles weren't formed by laughter, and she wore a frown instead of his usual intense and thoughtful smile. No. Her dad wasn't here. "Tina?"

Why did everyone say her name with a question mark attached? "Hello," Tina said in response. She had expected her grandmother to seem smaller, diminished somehow by age, but she was as tall and imposing as ever.

"I would have recognized you anywhere," Francine Nelson said. She had come from England as a young bride, and Tina still detected a slight British accent when she spoke. "You've grown up to look exactly as I had expected."

"What the hell is that supposed to mean?" Tina asked before she could stop herself. Too many memories of her grandmother's criticisms crowded into the greenhouse with the three of them. She was suddenly glad she hadn't gone back to the hotel to change. She wasn't here to impress anyone. "Oh, now I remember," she continued, her voice thick with sarcasm. "You always used to complain to Mom about what a mess I was."

"I meant to say you've turned into a stunning young woman. You needn't snap at me because I believed it was inappropriate for a child to come to the dinner table covered in mud."

"Nothing I did was ever proper enough for you."

Francine shook her head. "You and Peter could be twins. You look just like your father, but your temper is from your mother. It's all Irish."

"Don't you dare insult my mom," Tina said, her voice sounding like a protective growl in her own ears.

Only Peter's hand on her arm kept Tina in place. She felt the warmth of his touch through the sweater's wool. She didn't know whether she was about to storm out or fling herself over the table full of tomatoes and attack her grandmother. She felt a sense of disconnect, as if she were standing apart and watching her mom and grandmother fight. And her dad, trying to restore some peace. She leaned slightly into Peter's grasp.

"Gran, let's calm down and start over," he said. He frowned toward Francine. Tina would never be able to refer to her by such an endearing and familiar term as *Gran*. "Without any insults or racial slurs."

"She started it," Tina said at the exact moment as her grandmother. Jinx.

"I admit, your mother and I rarely agreed on how a child should be raised," Francine said after a short pause. "But, in spite of all our arguments, I cared for her. As the wife of my oldest son and the mother of my grandchild."

Tina heard the catch in her grandmother's voice when she spoke of her son, but Tina chose to ignore it. She had lost both parents. She didn't have room for pity. "If you cared so much, why weren't you around when Mom was sick?"

"I offered to move the two of you over here. She refused."

"She was ill. She needed peace and quiet, not someone nagging at her constantly." Tina crossed her arms over her chest, pulling away from Peter's hand. Her anger was only fueled with the knowledge that her grandmother was speaking the truth. And because she wasn't mentioning the money she had sent Tina to help cover the exorbitant fees charged by the hospice center. For some insane reason, her grandmother's refusal to defend herself by bringing up the one time she had been allowed to help Tina and her mom only made Tina more furious.

A customer wandered into the greenhouse, and Francine stepped closer. "What do you want from me, Tina?" she asked in a quiet voice.

It's not what I want now, but what I wanted then. Tina pictured her teenaged self as she took care of the house, cooked dinner, nursed her mom. Scared and alone. Coping with medical decisions and funeral arrangements instead of Saturday-night dates or softball games. Doing homework in hospital rooms, driving her mom to chemo treatments before she even had a license. With no family to turn to for comfort or help. Her grandmother had thrown some money at them, but it wasn't what Tina had needed.

"Nothing," she said. "I'm only here to help Peter because it's what Dad would have wanted. Then I'll go home."

"Very well," Francine said, her face an unreadable mask. "I'll leave you alone."

"As usual," Tina muttered as her grandmother walked away.

"I'm sorry," Peter said. He ran a hand through his hair. "Maybe we can sit down together for dinner sometime and—"

"Hey, Pete, don't worry about it," Tina said, torn between wanting to comfort him and wanting to get the hell out of there. "Why don't we just concentrate on the business? You said you had samples of the advertising you've done in the past."

"In my office," he said, gesturing toward the back of the lot, beyond the rows of greenhouses, and started walking. Tina followed him wearily. Five hours of driving and thirty years of anger were too much to handle in one day, and she desperately needed to get to the hotel. Her fingers twitched against her thighs as she walked. She needed her fiddle.

Peter unlocked a small shed and led her inside. It was dimly lit and barely big enough for the two of them and his small desk, which was as cluttered as his store and as messy as Tina's own work space at home. What little Tina could see of the wood desk was chipped and unstained oak, as organic and rooted in this place as the plants in the greenhouse, but most of its surface was covered with junk. She and Peter seemed to share more than just her father's looks. He pulled a file out from under several seed catalogs and balanced it on a chair.

Tina stopped him when he started to show her clippings from local papers. "I'm sure it's self-explanatory. Let me go over it this weekend, and we can get together Monday to review your budget and my ideas."

"Sure," he said as he handed her the thick file. "Do I need to give you an advance, or do I pay—"

"No," she said before he could finish. No way would she take money from her family and be in any way indebted to them. She had joked with Andy about double charging Peter and calling it compensation for hazardous duty, but after seeing him and her grandmother again, she knew she had to keep the freedom to walk away any time she wanted. No matter how little she could afford a summer without pay. She'd manage to pick up some odd jobs while she was here, to cover the few months of double rent. She had refused Peter's offer of his spare bedroom when she'd first agreed to come over, and she'd max out her credit cards at the hotel if necessary to keep her independence.

"I'm doing this for Dad," she said, to soften her sharp tone.

He walked her to the front of the store. "If you have time this weekend, I'd be glad to show you around the city. Or we can catch a movie…"

Tina held up the folder. "Thanks, but I have work to do. Plus, I have some projects I'm finishing up for other clients. But I'll be here Monday morning."

She turned away and hurried to the door, nearly tripping over a pile of garden hoses in her rush to get away.

❖

Tina barely paid attention to the opulence of the Davenport Hotel as she dragged herself and her bags to the registration counter. The recently renovated hotel was over a hundred years old and was the one bright and beautiful memory she had from all her childhood trips to Spokane. She paused by one of the huge, overstuffed maroon leather chairs in the lobby, tempted to snuggle into its depths like she had done years ago with her mother. But it looked too comfortable, and she looked too much like a vagrant. If she sat down, she'd either fall asleep or be booted to the curb.

Tina maneuvered herself, her three suitcases, and her fiddle into the old-fashioned elevator and waited for several moments before she realized she needed to use her room key card to make the doors shut and the elevator move. She swore under her breath as she fumbled through her pockets for the slim card. She had eleven floors to rest before she had to half drag, half carry her luggage down the long hallway. Her old Corolla didn't exactly rank with Fort Knox in terms of security, so she hadn't wanted to leave any of her belongings in the car. She dumped three months of clothes and toiletries and art supplies just inside the door before she carefully laid her fiddle case on the luggage rack.

She peered in the bathroom and groaned at the sight of the large waterfall-style shower. Elegant marble tiles and gold fixtures added to the ambience. She could almost feel the scalding water massaging her shoulders and rinsing the layers of dust and tension off her body. An oasis, private and waiting just for her.

It would have to wait a little longer. She usually wasn't a fan of delayed gratification, but she wanted to have her unpleasant to-do list finished before she let herself fully relax. She'd make the promised call to set up a meeting with Jan and then have a marathon shower and order one of everything from room service.

"Hello?" The voice answering Tina's call sounded harried and out of breath. She wondered briefly if she had interrupted Jan in the middle of sex. Would she be the type to stop and answer the phone?

"Is this Jan? I'm Tina, Brooke and Andy's friend."

"Oh, hi. I'm glad you called. Did you have a good trip?"

Tina smiled. Jan didn't *sound* glad. She sounded annoyed. Maybe she'd be just as willing as Tina to meet once, drink a sarcastic toast to Brooke, and then never see each other again.

"Long and boring, thanks for asking. Hey, I have some free time this weekend before I have to settle into my job, so I thought we could meet for drinks tomorrow night."

"Tomorrow night…That'll be fine. I'll make it work."

Try to contain your enthusiasm. "Great. About nine? In the Peacock Room at the Davenport?" Tina had spotted the bar on her way into the hotel. Fussy and formal and full of people in business attire. It seemed designed for casual meetings between acquaintances and totally unsuited for long romantic trysts. The ideal way to set the tone for a hopefully brief meeting.

"Sure…What? The Peacock Room?"

"Yes. Is that okay?" Tina asked impatiently. She wondered how she'd make it through an hour with Jan when she could barely tolerate one short phone call. Maybe the alcohol would help.

"Yes. It's just not the kind of place I expected you to pick."

Tina heard the slight emphasis on *you*. What the hell was that about? "I'm staying at the Davenport for a few days, so it's the only bar I know."

There was a long pause. Tina glanced at her phone to make sure she hadn't been disconnected. "We're meeting in a bar in your hotel?" Jan finally asked. Tina could sense some kind of emotion behind the words, but she couldn't read it clearly. Horror? Disgust? What exactly had Brooke and Andy said about her?

"You'll be perfectly safe," she said, her words clipped. "I promise not to ravish you in the lobby or lure you to my room."

"That's not what I—"

"Besides, I've invited my cousin to join us. He'll make sure you're safe from me."

"No, it's just…Brooke told me you were staying for a few months, so I didn't expect you to be living in a hotel. That sounds very expensive."

"It's only temporary, until I find an apartment or something," Tina said. Or something. Like ditching the whole stupid plan and getting the hell out of Spokane.

"You mean you came here without arranging for a place to *live*?"

Tina could hear Jan's disbelief even over the phone. She was certain Jan was the type to have every aspect of her life planned, down to the minutest detail. "I like to be spontaneous," she said. By spontaneous, she meant foolish and poor. Paying rent on her Seattle apartment and racking up bills in a fancy hotel. She made decent money at her job, but she could only afford to live in one city at a time. But she wasn't about to admit any of that to Jan.

"Well, I'm sure something will come up," Jan said, sounding about as convinced as Tina was.

"Something always does. Say, I think I hear room service at the door," Tina lied. She needed to get off the phone. Now.

"Okay. See you tomorrow."

Tina ended the call and dropped onto the bed. That went well. And now she had to call Peter and invite him for drinks. Suddenly, a shower and meal didn't seem strong enough to erase the stress of the day. Instead, she opened her fiddle case and took out her instrument. She ran a hand over the carved maple, shaped into the barest outline of a violin and painted flame red. She untangled the mess of cords and plugged her headphones into the violin so she could play as loudly as she wanted and no one else could hear. Volume on high.

She started with a simple Scottish tune about bluebonnets, her mom's favorite lullaby. She played it again, over and over, adding embellishments and trills and double stops. Blending in bits of other songs, changing keys. Improvising until the song was her own, until she was back in control, until she had played out all her feelings except hunger. Only then did she stop playing and order dinner.

❖

Jan hung up and perched on a kitchen stool. Tina had managed to catch her at the worst possible moment. She had been moving her dad's belongings into her master suite—with its dormer windows and cozy reading nook and high ceilings—and her own things into the small spare bedroom upstairs. He'd need the extra space and the en suite bathroom while he recovered. She didn't care about the size of the room and she wanted her father to be comfortable, but it was yet another unsettling change in a long series of them.

She had raced to get the phone, expecting a call from the doctor, and managed to bang her shin on the coffee table hard enough to make her want to kill someone. Anyone. She had struggled to control her breathing and her temper while she half listened to Tina, and the mention of a hotel bar had caught her off guard, her thoughts unprotected. Most of the fantasies she had concocted about Tina during Brooke's botched wedding weekend had started exactly that way. Except *she* was the one who called Tina and invited her for a drink in *her* hotel's bar. What happened after that—whether in the hall, on the elevator, or in her room—varied, but the overture was constant.

Hearing her fantasies echoed in Tina's voice had been too much to take, and Jan realized she would have to be vigilant and not let her libido take control. She was stressed by all the recent changes, and even considering a relationship that promised only to be temporary and inconstant was ridiculous. Thank God, Tina's cousin would be there. Even so, she picked up the phone again and called Chloe. There'd be safety in numbers, the more the better.

CHAPTER FOUR

Tina sat alone in the Peacock Room, sipping a Jameson on the rocks and rocking her heel in time to the down-bow of a fiddle tune that played in her mind. She had told Jan she chose the Davenport's bar because it was conveniently located in the hotel, but she secretly loved the ambience of the stuffy room. At first glance, it looked elegant and grand, with wood paneling, brocade-covered walls, and granite-topped tables. The peacock-inspired royals, purples, and deep greens in the fabrics and paint blended smoothly with the dark wood tones and rich leather chairs. But closer inspection revealed the truth. The patterned carpet was worn, the gilded fixtures looked inexpertly spray painted, and the cracked edges of the granite and wood furnishings exposed them as nothing more than veneer. Patrons were invited to stay a short time, enjoy the illusion of depth and luxury, and then move on. Stay on the surface. Exactly the tone Tina wanted to set for the evening.

She wasn't looking forward to socializing with her cousin, but he had sounded pleased to be invited. She hoped three would, indeed, prove to be a crowd, and Peter's presence would keep the conversation from turning personal. And, likewise, Jan's presence would keep Peter from asking Tina about her thoughts regarding his business, because she wasn't prepared to answer him yet. She had been determined to spend the afternoon planning her PR campaign for his nursery, but instead, she had played her violin most of the day.

The bar's name had triggered a nagging memory, and she had searched online until she found someone playing Winston Fitzgerald's version of the Cape Breton fiddle tune "Peacock's Fancy." She'd listened to the interpretation and mimicked it on her own fiddle before starting to add her own flair, and then she'd combined her version with the air about bluebonnets she had been playing the night before. A few happy hours later, she had the grace notes and accents just right, and the new medley was her own. Now, she rehearsed it in her mind while she waited, adding tapping fingers to the beat of her heel as she rethought the bridge between the two tunes.

Andy always looked a little nervous when Tina talked about changing melodies or notes in her music. Classical music was more Andy's style, and Tina appreciated her ability to pull nuance and meaning out of the notes *exactly* as they were written. But the old fiddle tunes Tina loved best had been passed down by ear from generation to generation, changing with each person who played them, belonging to no one and everyone at once. She was free to alter them to fit her style and her mood, but she never felt more connected to her family than she did when she played an old Irish jig or reel. Connected to her mother's side of the family, of course. She'd rather forget any ties she had to the other side.

"Are you dancing?"

Tina jumped in surprise. She'd been so caught up in her song she hadn't noticed Peter approaching the table, and she hadn't realized she was noticeably moving to her own beat. He seemed seriously concerned for her sanity, and she was tempted to play along. Dancing by herself in the middle of a bar ought to confirm the rumor that she was the off-kilter black sheep of the family.

"Oh, sit down. I'm not going to embarrass you," she said in exasperation. "I spent the day practicing on my violin, and the song is stuck in my head."

Peter sat across from her. He looked at home in the bar, with his navy suit and open-collared pale blue shirt. She was about to tease him for dressing too formally for a simple drink with friends, but she didn't look any more casual. She had justified the effort of getting her black wool-blend slacks and red silk tank dry-cleaned and pressed this afternoon because she had been so scruffy the day before. Peter was putting the reputation of his business in her hands, and she wanted him to see that she cleaned up just fine. And, she had to admit, she liked the thought of looking her best when Jan saw her. She never put much effort into dressing for other women. She just showed up as herself, and no one had ever seemed disappointed. She wondered, briefly, why meeting Jan seemed different, but she didn't want to examine the question too deeply.

"Glad to hear it. You seemed a bit…tense yesterday."

"It was a long fucking drive," Tina said, doing her best to warn him off the topic with her tone.

Peter just laughed. "Yeah, with Gran at the end of it." He quickly changed the subject. "I should have known you'd be musical. Our whole family is."

"My grandpa on Mom's side was a fiddle player and music professor. That's where I get it," Tina said stiffly.

"I know. Your dad studied with him at WSU, where he met Aunt Kathleen. I mean, your mom. But we all play something. Piano for Dad and Gran, clarinet for Mom, oboe for my sister."

Tina had a flash of recognition while he spoke. Christmas. She must have been four or five. She could picture Uncle Nick at the piano, with everyone gathered around him singing and laughing. She shrugged it off. One happy memory did not a family make.

"So what about you?" she asked, twirling her drink so the melting ice chinked against the glass. "What's your musical poison?"

"Um, I played french horn in high school and college. I haven't kept up with it, though."

Tina leaned her elbows on the table. He was a stranger to her, yet his mannerisms and expressions were too familiar. Too like her own. "You hesitated. Do you play something else, something I'll think is funny? Panpipes? Bass guitar in a heavy-metal band? Are you a one-man band with a little monkey?"

"Mandolin," Peter admitted. "I'm in a period group, and we play all the local Renaissance fairs, Shakespeare in the Park, that sort of thing. And I'm so glad I could amuse you."

Tina wiped her eyes and tried to control her laughter. The idea of prim and proper Peter strolling around in leggings and a feathered cap was too funny. "Even better than I imagined," she said.

"Mock all you want, we have a great time. You should join us sometime this summer. We can always use another fiddle. And a few of us play at a pub called O'Boyle's every Tuesday night if you want to come meet the gang."

Tina's laughter faded a bit. O'Boyle's was the pub she had noticed on her way to the nursery. So much for the hope she had found a private place to enjoy music and maybe some female companionship. Neither would be as much fun with her cousin hovering nearby.

"Hey, is that your friend?"

Tina had been distracted by her conversation with Peter, and she had forgotten about Jan. She turned in her chair and saw two women in the doorway. Jan. She hadn't changed much in two years. Her hair was longer, curling slightly and hanging just past her shoulders, and she was wearing dark jeans and a white shirt, sheer enough to barely show the outline of her bra, instead of the silk outfit she had worn to Brooke's rehearsal. But, otherwise, she looked the same. The gold tones in her dark blond hair made the gilded fixtures appear even shabbier by comparison, and her intense eyes—the same deep, washed blue as her jeans—seemed to be analyzing and measuring everything they saw.

"Yep," Tina said as she waved at Jan. She fought hard to keep from looking anywhere below Jan's chin.

"Wow. She is absolutely gorgeous."

The wistful note in Peter's voice was enough to make Tina turn away from the sight of Jan walking toward their table.

"Yes, she is. And she's gay. I thought I made that clear."

"The brunette? I mean, I know your friend is gay, but isn't she the blonde?"

Tina turned again to the two women as they neared the table. Sure enough, the other woman was a brunette. Tina hadn't noticed.

Jan watched the exchange between Tina and her cousin as she led Chloe to the table in the back of the bar. Tina was frowning, and Jan wondered if she was about to interrupt an argument. Brooke had mentioned Tina's estrangement from her family, so she had been surprised to hear a cousin would be joining them. It didn't look like a happy family reunion. Great. An unwanted invitation to drinks and a family argument as a bonus. At least the cousin didn't look as angry as Tina did. In fact, he looked mesmerized as he stared past Jan as if she didn't exist. Straight at Chloe.

No one seemed inclined to speak first, so Jan decided to start. "It's nice to finally meet you, Tina," she said, reaching out her hand. Tina hesitated before she shook it. The first touch. Jan had imagined how Tina's hands would feel way too many times over the past two years. A firm grip with soft hands, long and slender fingers wrapped around her own. The warmth of reality felt much better than anything her imagination had created. She pulled back a little too quickly. Barely enough of a handshake to be polite, let alone to be affected by Tina's touch. "This is my friend Chloe."

"Oh, your *friend*. I thought maybe you hired a bodyguard for the occasion," Tina said, nodding at Chloe. "I take it you didn't feel safe with me even with Peter here to protect your virtue."

Jan stood still, unable to think of a retort. Had Tina read her mind? Did she somehow know about Jan's fantasy of meeting like this and letting herself be seduced?

"What Tina meant to say is please, have a seat. And she'd like to introduce her cousin, Peter," Peter said, with a frown in Tina's direction. She stuck her tongue out at him, but he ignored her and stood up, pulling out a chair for Chloe. "What can I get you to drink?"

"I like red wine," Chloe said. "Do they have anything from the Spokane Valley?"

"They serve a nice Latah Creek merlot. It's one of my personal favorites," Peter said.

"Then I'm sure I'll love it."

"Excellent. I'll have the same. I try to support local producers whenever possible."

"Drink local, and drink often," Chloe said. She and Peter laughed at the joke.

"I'll have a scotch and soda," Jan said.

"Okay," Peter said briefly. He went to the bar, leaving Chloe staring after him like a love-struck teenager. Jan rolled her eyes at Tina.

"Do you think he even heard me?" she asked.

"He's cute," Chloe said at the same time. "So, is he single?" she asked Tina.

"I doubt it," Tina said in Jan's direction. "And I think so, but I really don't keep up on his love life," she said to Chloe.

"Really? Pickup lines like those, and he's *single*?" Jan muttered. "Hard to believe."

"No shit," Tina said. She leaned toward Jan. "Hey, baby, maybe we should order an appetizer," she spoke in an uncanny imitation of her cousin's voice. "They have nachos—my personal favorite."

"I'm sure I'll love anything you love," Jan answered, matching the seductive tone of Tina's voice. "And I've heard the cheese is locally sourced."

"Ooh, that is so hot," Tina said before she broke into laughter. Jan joined in, surprised by this teasing side of Tina. Jan had only been in the same room with her two times, but already she could see something so unrestrained about Tina, whether she was flirting or irritated or joking. Every expression played across her face, as if uncensored. Jan could never let herself be so open. And she definitely shouldn't find the trait so appealing.

Chloe crossed her arms over her chest while they laughed. "Shut up, both of you, or I'll…I'll call your friend Brooke."

"And tell her what?" Tina asked, looking unconcerned as she polished off her drink.

"I'll tell her I definitely saw a spark between the two of you, and I think you'll fall in love if she just pushes you together more."

Jan stopped laughing as quickly as Tina did. "You wouldn't dare," she said to Chloe. She realized she sounded horrified by the suggestion, and she turned to Tina. "No offense."

"None taken," Tina said with a casual shrug. She looked slowly up and down Jan's body. "You're not exactly my type, either."

Jan knew she shouldn't care if Tina didn't want her. Shouldn't care if Tina's gaze seemed to take in her body and her personality, and find both of them lacking. But the rejection hurt more than she expected, and she spoke without thinking. "So what *is* your type? Someone with no morals and a couple hours to spare?"

"Sure beats uptight and frigid."

Peter returned with four glasses precariously balanced in his hands. "Here we are," he said. "Tina, I got you another drink while I was…Is something wrong?"

"Of course not," Chloe said, reaching out to help him with the glasses. "We were just talking about work. I was telling Tina that I teach French at Spokane Heights."

"Really? I spent a semester in Paris when I was in college. Let me see if I can remember anything…"

The two of them started chatting in French, obviously unconcerned about Jan's and Tina's inability to follow the conversation. Jan listened to Peter's stilted phrases and Chloe's laughter-laced corrections. She had invited Chloe to help her keep the conversation with Tina casual, not to distract the only other neutral person at the table. She was frustrated. She continued to make plans, but other people seemed inclined to disregard them.

"I think we lost them," Tina said with a sigh, leaning back in her chair and taking a sip of her fresh drink.

"Seems that way," Jan said. She ran the tip of her finger over her glass, drawing a tessellation of triangles in the condensation. "I'm sorry I snapped at you. I'm just not looking for a relationship right now, and Brooke can be, well, persistent."

Mesmerized, Tina watched Jan's finger trace a series of shapes. "Obsessive," she suggested.

"Crazy," Jan added with a small grin. "Especially if she thinks there's a chance we're going to get along. We seem so different."

"And we barely made it five minutes before we were insulting each other," Tina said. She stared blankly at the table behind Jan, anything to keep from gawking at her. And the way her fingertip kept moving slowly over her wet glass.

Jan glanced over her shoulder and then looked back at Tina with raised eyebrows. "Go ahead and talk to them if you want. I don't want to cramp your style."

"What?" Tina asked, confused until she realized she had been staring at a table full of women wearing business outfits and name tags. Most likely at the hotel for a convention. On a typical day, she would already have singled out her choice and would be about to make her move. But tonight she felt too tired to stage a seduction scene. "Don't worry about it," she said dismissively, turning her attention back to Jan and struggling to find a pleasant, or at least neutral, topic. "Do you like teaching?"

"I love it. The Heights is a wonderful school—very progressive, and the kids are great."

"I might be more convinced if you weren't frowning so hard," Tina joked, trying to coax Jan back into the playful mood she had been in earlier. When her laughter had instantaneously erased the seriousness of her expression. Jan looked like she was carrying the weight of her world alone, and Tina had at first assumed she was naturally gloomy and humorless. But the burst of laughter had been spontaneous and genuine—a sure sign there was passion and fun under her stuffy exterior. What problems sat so heavily on her? Tina reached out and gently traced the crease between Jan's brows. She meant to distract herself from wondering about Jan's personal life, but the soft brush of Jan's bangs against her finger made her snatch her hand back.

"My dad is sick, and I might need to move so he can be near the right VA hospital," Jan said without thinking. She faltered to a halt. Why was she telling Tina this? One brief, meaningless touch and she was pouring out her secrets? Chloe had stopped her little French lesson and was watching her. Jan hadn't shared this much with her, and she had known Chloe for two years. Jan shrugged in what she hoped was a nonchalant manner. "I'll be able to find another job, of course, and I'm lucky to have started my teaching career at a school like this one."

"The school is lucky to have a teacher like you," Chloe said quietly, bumping Jan with her shoulder. She raised her voice to a normal level. "Jan's students love her, too. And she's the advisor for the GLBTQ group. She's been a great advocate for them, and there'll be several same-sex couples at the prom."

Jan could feel her face heat when everyone at the table turned their attention on her. She was proud of her efforts to help the students not only feel safe, but feel included at school. Her own high school wouldn't have been so accepting, but it hadn't been an issue for her since her dad had been transferred to a different base, in a different country, toward the end of her senior year. She hadn't cared about missing the prom, but she had hated leaving Claire, her first girlfriend, after only one short month together. She hadn't done much dating since then. She didn't want to fall in love again until she could be sure she wouldn't be wrested away.

"It shouldn't be such a big deal to go to a silly dance, gay or straight," she said. She wanted to push the focus off her, and Tina seemed to be a good target. "You went to school in Seattle, didn't you, Tina? Could you be out there?"

Tina shrugged and stared at the empty glass in her hands. "Actually, I have no idea. I didn't date in high school, let alone go to the prom."

"Don't tell me a knockout like you couldn't get a date," Chloe said in a teasing voice.

"My mom was very sick from her chemo treatments during most of my senior year. I barely managed to graduate, let alone do any extracurricular activities."

Jan felt a sudden, ridiculous urge to reach for Tina, understanding completely how it felt to be caretaker for an ailing parent, but she stopped herself. Instead, Peter covered Tina's hand. Tina seemed to accept the contact for a brief moment, and then she pulled away.

"I'm sorry," Chloe said. "I didn't know. But it's never too late. Jan and I are chaperones, so we were planning to go together, but I told her it would mean a lot to the kids if she went with a date." She paused, and then smiled brightly. "Hey, the two of you should go as a couple."

Jan, shocked, started to reason her way out of this mess. "There is no way—"

"Are you fucking insane?" Tina interrupted, rising out of the casual, slouched pose she had been in all evening.

"Wonderful," Peter said, more loudly than either Jan or Tina. "It's settled. And if you'll allow me to escort you, Chloe, we can make it a double date."

The conversation dwindled after Peter's pronouncement, but he and Chloe made a valiant effort to keep everyone talking. Jan was caught between stunned disbelief at their suggestion and a crazy desire to laugh at the expression on Tina's face. She looked disgusted, as if she'd been drafted to swim across a sewage plant, not go to a dance. Jan decided she herself might have opted for the first if she had a choice. All she'd wanted was to get through the evening as quickly and impersonally as possible. A reluctant prom date hadn't been part of the plan. She searched wildly for a way to back out, but she had to go to the dance. For her kids. Tina would have to be the one to make an escape, and Jan figured she'd be so practiced at breaking dates it would be easy for her. She probably had a thousand handy excuses at the ready.

"Worst safety net *ever*," Jan whispered to Chloe when Peter and Tina went to the bar for another round.

Chloe smiled. "It seemed like the best way to get him to ask me out."

Jan glanced at the two cousins who seemed to be having a similar conversation at the bar. "So you used me?" she asked, shocked by Chloe's manipulation. She hadn't gotten close to Chloe over the years they'd been teaching together, and she had simply thought of her as a very nice, but sort of bland person. She was definitely more interesting—albeit annoying—than Jan had expected.

"Well, you used me first, to be your third wheel. I'm just better at the game than you are," Chloe said, looking decidedly unrepentant. She laughed and bumped Jan again. "Besides, it's obvious one of you will find a way to get out of going. But I'll still have my date, so everyone wins."

Jan didn't quite see how she had won anything, but she stayed silent. In fact, she was out a date to the dance since she had planned on hanging out with Chloe for the evening. She supposed she'd end up going to the prom with the predatory Sasha. Ah well, worse things had happened.

Tina interrupted her musings when she set a drink in front of her. Jan thanked her and bit back an urge to ask how much she owed for it. She didn't want it to seem like a date, but she also didn't want to make a prudish fuss about money. "Why don't I order us some appetizers?" she asked instead.

"I should warn you," Tina said, once they had been served. She leaned toward Jan over their shared plate of tempura vegetables, glaring at Chloe and Peter, who had retreated to their corner of the table, as isolated as if a wall had been erected between the two couples. "If they start feeding each other, I'm going to throw up on the table."

"I'll probably join you," Jan said with a shrug, eating a crispy fried spear of broccoli rabe. "I have to apologize. I had no idea Chloe was such a flirt."

"Yeah, but it's my cousin's parody of Casanova that makes me want to puke."

"I agree. You know, they're as bad as Brooke. It's one thing to want a relationship for yourself, but to force innocent bystanders into them, too? It's not right."

"I agree," Tina said, looking surprised by the revelation. "Do your own disgusting flirting. But leave those of us who aren't interested in any serious commitments alone."

"Well," Jan said with a frown as she ate some cauliflower. "I wouldn't say I don't want a partner. But I'm waiting for the right time, and the right person."

Tina shrugged and spilt the last fried zucchini in half, giving one piece to Jan. "Not me. I'm not interested in being tied down. Ever. To anyone."

Jan ate the zucchini in silence. She was tempted to say something about Tina's dating habits, but it would only send them circling back to the earlier, insult-filled portion of the evening. They agreed they wanted to be left alone. She should accept the slight bit of camaraderie and leave the rest. Take her own advice, and let Tina make her own choices. Temporary and insubstantial as they were.

"So. Geometry," Tina said, wiping her greasy fingers on a burgundy cloth napkin. "What a thrilling subject. I vaguely remember something about pi from my high-school class."

"Actually, it's quite fascinating, especially when you get past the basics," Jan said, unperturbed by Tina's dismissal of her field as uninteresting. She was used to the attitude—in fact, she faced it square on at the beginning of every semester. "There are some interesting studies being conducted about the connections between geometric forms and music."

"Really?" Tina asked. "I've heard of mathematical principles associated with Bach's works, but I never got how numbers and shapes had anything to do with music."

"Hey, Chloe," Jan called across the divided table. "Do you have a pencil? And something to write on. Thanks." She turned Chloe's shopping list over and started to sketch. "So let's start with a simple scale."

"In what key?" Tina asked. Jan waved her hand vaguely.

"I don't know. Pick one," she said. "It's not important."

Tina coughed as she choked on a sip of her whiskey. "Not important? Are you kidding?"

❖

"Hey, Jan." Chloe interrupted the heated discussion Jan and Tina were having about atonal music.

"What?" Jan asked, holding the pencil out of reach as Tina tried to grab it.

"I should get going. It's getting kind of late."

"Really?" Tina asked, sounding as surprised as Jan was when she checked her watch. She and Tina had been talking for over two hours.

"Oh, sorry," Jan said, gathering her coat and getting up. "I didn't realize. I need to get home to check on Dad. Well, this was fun."

"It was," Tina agreed, standing up and shaking her hand quickly. "We should try not to do it again sometime."

Her tone was teasing, though, and Jan laughed as she put on her coat and said good-bye. Peter had gallantly, and annoyingly, offered to walk them to the car, and Jan expected Tina would take this opportunity to go after one of the single women in the bar. Instead, Jan watched her head straight to the elevators without a backward glance. The plan to have two neutral people there as buffers had failed, but they had managed to get through the evening with only limited insults and with no public scenes. Brooke would just have to be satisfied with small victories.

CHAPTER FIVE

Jan was halfway across the hotel lobby when she spotted Tina curled up in an oversized leather chair, a book on her lap and a paper coffee cup on the table next to her. Jan barely recognized her—she looked so different from the slick, sexy woman of the night before. No less sexy, of course, but her beige sweater looked moth-devoured and her jeans were faded, with frayed seams along her calves and thighs. She wasn't reading but was watching Jan walk toward her, an unreadable expression on her face.

The chairs were placed in square-shaped groupings of four. Jan sat in the one next to Tina and sighed as she nestled into its depths and felt herself relax. She had left her house to give her dad some time to himself after she'd spent the morning following him around and overreacting every time he seemed remotely confused. They were both going to need time to adjust to the situation, and she needed to learn how to help him without taking away his dignity. So she had come in search of Tina, but she wasn't sure how to ask for help. She looked around the lobby while Tina continued to watch her in silence. The arch-ceilinged room was inlayed and adorned to the hilt. Where the ornate carpet ended, marble tiles began. A fountain with a statue of cupid decorated the center of the room, its bowl filled with large flowers.

"We have our year-end student award ceremony in one of the ballrooms upstairs," Jan said, gesturing toward the balcony. "I've always loved this place. It's a bit gaudier than my usual style, but it works here."

Tina hesitated a moment before speaking. "We stayed here every time we came to see my dad's parents," she said, staring up at a chandelier. "Mom and I would sit down here, and she'd tell me stories about what the hotel was like when she used to come here when she was young."

Jan watched Tina's expression soften as she talked, and she wondered, briefly, what was in the coffee cup that was making her seem so open and friendly. She figured it was simply the effect of memories, drawn close to the surface by the nostalgia of the place.

"She said there were gold birdcages hanging in the arches, and each one had a colored parakeet in it. And there were bellmen who wore burgundy uniforms with gold braid and little boxy hats, and sometimes one of them would take out a parakeet and have it sing for her. And up there"—Tina pointed to the center balustrade, but Jan didn't follow the gesture. She couldn't take her eyes off Tina, but she could see the room transformed through the two generations of stories—"there was a glass case with a stuffed polar bear inside. I used to have dreams about that bear coming to get me, and I'd ride on his back to the Arctic."

"And now you're back."

Tina returned to the present, her voice taking on an edgy quality. "Now I'm back. And I'm still waiting for that damned bear to rescue me."

"You don't seem surprised to see me here."

"I figured you wouldn't be able to resist my charms for long," Tina said with a laugh. "Plus, I knew you'd get in touch with me sooner or later about backing out of the whole prom thing."

"You're right about the second one, at least," Jan said. She might have some trouble with the first, but she would manage to resist. She had to. Life was shaky enough without adding an unsettling, temporary affair to the mix. "But it's not why I'm here. I've come to offer you a place to live while you're in town."

Tina stared at Jan while she decided how to respond. Move in with Jan? No way. But for a very brief moment she wanted to say okay and drag Jan out the door. She could come back for her things later. "A couple days ago you sounded afraid to meet me alone in my hotel's lobby, but now you're asking me to move in with you? I must have been extra charming last night."

"Not with me," Jan said, enunciating each word clearly, as if she wanted to leave no doubt in Tina's mind about her intentions. "And, trust me, you weren't even moderately charming. But my dad hurt his shoulder, so he'll be staying with me for a few weeks, at least. He said you could use his apartment. It's only a fifteen-minute drive from your cousin's place, so you'd have an easy commute."

Tina felt a wave of relief at the suggestion. The prospect of searching for housing had been unpleasant, and she didn't know what she'd have to settle for since she wasn't signing a long-term lease. "Wow, that'd be great. I'll pay rent, of course."

"Well, instead of rent, I was hoping you might do a favor for me. And for my dad."

Tina watched Jan shift in her chair, and she looked like she was chewing the inside of her lip. Tina wondered if this had something to do with her dad's sickness Jan had mentioned the night before, when she'd shown similar signs of tension and worry. Tina leaned forward and gave Jan's knee an awkward squeeze. "Hey, what is it? What do you need?"

Instead of reassuring Jan, Tina's gesture seemed to upset her more. Her eyes reddened as if she was about to cry, and Tina had the sinking feeling she was about to say yes to any favor Jan asked. But only because Brooke and Andy would expect her to help, of course.

"My dad might have early onset Alzheimer's. His symptoms are still slight, and very manageable, but his doctor made a few suggestions about keeping his mind active. He said things like looking at pictures or listening to familiar music would help keep his memories intact longer."

Tina let her hand rest gently on Jan's knee again. Jan would have to watch her father slowly forget the life they'd shared. Tina remembered the deep loneliness she'd felt after losing her mother. But she had never doubted that her mom remembered and cherished their time together.

"How can I help?" Tina asked. *I'll do anything*, she meant. This time, she didn't even try to pretend she was only helping the friend of a friend. Still, it was only common decency, and hardly personal, to feel compassion for someone in Jan's situation.

Jan sniffed and rubbed the back of her hand over her eyes. "I've seen some of the sites you've created, for your quartet and for Brooke's catering business, and I admire the way you blend images and music. Dad has tons of pictures and old records in the apartment. I thought maybe you could make a slide show on a DVD with some of his favorite songs, or something like that."

"Smart idea. Combining visual and auditory triggers ought to help his memory," Tina said, her mind racing ahead of the conversation and into the planning phase of the project and how she would connect the images. Not simply chronologically, she decided, but she'd have to find unique thematic threads, so the slide show would be more interesting. And therefore more memorable. "I'll do it."

"Thank you," Jan said. Tina saw some of the tension in Jan's jaw release as she smiled with apparent relief. Tina understood all too well what it was like to be alone and caring for an ill parent. She would help Jan in this small way, but she'd be glad not to have a share in any future responsibility. She wasn't going to play caretaker again for anyone, sick or healthy.

Jan held out a printed sheet of paper and a single key on a blue-and-red Gonzaga key chain. "Here are directions to the apartment. I already cleared out some space in the closet and the top drawers of Dad's dresser for you. I have parent-teacher conferences the first part of the week, so I'll give you a chance to get settled. Maybe I could come over Thursday evening and show you the photos?"

Apparently Jan had assumed she'd say yes. Tina felt her breath constrict slightly as if a chain were being tightened around her. She recognized her typical response to a new, unwanted obligation. She took a deep breath and let the sensation pass before she reached out and accepted the apartment key. "I'll be there," she said.

❖

Tina checked out of the Davenport Monday morning and drove the now-familiar route to Peter's nursery. She hated to leave the huge bed with its pillowy mattress and spotless white linens, the amazing shower, the memories of her parents. She shouldn't have shared so much personal information with Jan, but she hadn't been able to stop the words from flowing out. She had been in the lobby, while her mocha grew cold and her book sat unread, missing her parents and fiddling absently with the gold brooch she had pinned on her sweater. Bought for her in the hotel's gift shop by her mom, it was shaped like a treble clef and had a small ruby set in the curl. It had seemed impossibly grown-up and fancy to a child of eight, and Tina had treasured the gift. Even more as she grew older, since her dad had died shortly after what was to be their last trip to Spokane. For a moment, the Davenport of her mother's childhood had seemed more tangible than the present-day hotel, and she could see the bellmen and birdcages, hear the twittering song of the parakeets. When Jan had sat beside her, the old stories had simply needed to be shared.

Jan. Bearing the good news of a practically free apartment for the summer. Tina should feel relieved—at least her credit cards were—but she was wary, instead. She had been noncommittal about the three-month sojourn in Spokane. She'd told everyone she would stay, but she had always kept the possibility of an escape in her mind. Having her housing dilemma settled so easily only helped cement her presence in this place. And now, instead of one unpleasant personal obligation, she had two. She had quit a well-paying job in a design firm to work freelance mainly because she disliked taking orders from a boss. How much worse to work for a family she barely acknowledged and an uptight schoolteacher who seemed edgy around her, as if Tina might jump her bones at any moment. As if. She made it a point of personal principle to avoid overly responsible, settled women like Jan, especially ones with uncertain and stressful futures as caretakers. Jan might be sexy as hell, and Tina might be tempted to hone in on the tension Jan carried in her shoulders and lips—smoothing Jan's worries away with her touch and her kiss—but she wouldn't let any physical attraction overcome common sense.

She'd share her talent as an artist with these two clients because she had promised to do so. But she'd keep her heart and soul well away from them both.

Tina parked in the nursery lot. She'd get her meeting with Peter over with before she'd settle in the apartment. The neighborhood seemed safe enough, but she carried her fiddle case with her. She didn't care if someone stole all her clothes, but she didn't want to risk losing her instrument. She warily watched for any sign of her grandmother and made it to Peter's office without seeing her.

"She's not here today," Peter said from the doorway of his shed. He must have noticed her glancing furtively around the lot.

"Who's not here?" Tina asked, keeping her tone neutral even though the feelings Francine inspired were anything but.

"You know, she hardly ever comes to the shop unless she needs something for her garden. She stayed all day last week because she knew you were arriving."

"Oh, goody. How kind of her to make a special trip just for the chance to criticize me."

"That's not…" Peter made a gesture of surrender and dropped the subject. Tina decided her glare must have been particularly effective. She'd have to remember that particular scowl for the next time he brought up a subject she didn't like.

"Your violin will be safe here," he said after he cleared space on a shelf and gave it a quick dust. Tina carefully set her fiddle down, pushing away the recognition his nonchalant action stirred in her. Only another musician would take it for granted she didn't want to leave her instrument alone in the car.

"So you're moving into Jan's father's apartment today?" he asked as they settled at the small desk. He had brought a second chair into the cramped toolshed. "Don't snarl at me. Jan told Chloe this morning, and she told me when I met her for lunch."

"*That* grapevine didn't take long to grow," Tina muttered. Great. Now the chain was complete. She wouldn't be able to make a move in this town without her entire network knowing. She took a folder out of her backpack and thumped it on the desk. "Do you mind if we spend more time on work and less on gossip?"

"Mentioning your name in a conversation is *not* gossip."

"Was I there to defend myself? Didn't think so. Now look at these color swatches before I stuff them up your nose."

"Ouch," Peter said, scooting his chair a few inches away from hers. He held his hands in front of his face as if to ward her off, but Tina could still see the humor in his eyes. "I remember you did that to Lindsay. I never could play with those toy soldiers again after knowing where they'd been."

Tina tried to keep from joining his laughter, but she finally gave in. His brat of a little sister had had it coming, but none of the adults had agreed. "Too bad she's in Chicago. I'd have liked to see her again."

"I spoke to her on the phone a few days ago, and she sends her love. She's a very forgiving soul."

Tina's laughter ended with a sigh. Leave it to Peter to dredge up one of her happier memories. She seemed to have forgotten most of them. "Okay, we've gossiped and reminisced. *Now* can we get down to business? I have a few ideas for color schemes and print styles. Once you choose a general look for the business, I can adapt it to your various marketing tools."

Tina spent over an hour with him, combining different fonts and palettes until he seemed pleased with the effect. When Peter had first contacted her, he'd asked for a complete PR package instead of the simple web design she usually offered. She had been tempted to say she wasn't qualified, find someone else, but then she'd spent a few days considering the possibility of expanding her freelance business. He wanted her to design everything—from print ads to curtains for trade-show booths to seasonal in-store promotions—and unlike any nonfamily client, he didn't care how qualified she was. She would come away from the experience with a brochure full of new services she could offer. It had seemed worth the sacrifice of a few short weeks.

She tapped her pages of notes on the desk until the edges were even and slid them into the folder. "Do you have the measurements for your booth at the home-and-garden show?" Peter hunted for the information in his stacks of papers, and she added it to her file. "I'll come up with a few ideas for the drapes and tablecloths and bring them to you by the end of the week. Once you choose, I'll get the order in, so we can get them made in time for the show. Then I'll get to work on the website."

She hooked her backpack over one shoulder and picked up her violin case. "I'll give you a call before I show up. Or maybe Chloe can let you know."

"Ha-ha." He walked with her to the Corolla. "Do you want to come to O'Boyle's tomorrow night? It's an open session if you want to play, or you can just listen."

The offer was tempting. The fiddle was meant to be played with other people, not alone in her room, and she already missed the fellowship she felt with Andy and other musicians in her network back home. "I really need to get some work done and get settled in the apartment," she said, fastening a seat belt over her case. "But maybe next week."

CHAPTER SIX

Jan pulled a pan of herb-roasted red potatoes out of the oven and gingerly scooped them into a serving bowl using just the tips of her fingers. She licked her fingertips to soothe the slight burn and to taste the warmth of oil and thyme. Perfect. She felt grounded after cooking, although the feeling rarely lasted long. The visions of good food, a family gathered around a table, shared conversation spiced by shared flavors and smells. She longed for a life full of such moments, but she was willing to take the occasional hour here and there.

"Dinner's ready, Dad," she called as she balanced the bowl of potatoes in one hand and a platter of sliced meatloaf in the other.

"Smells great, pumpkin," Glen said as he walked into the kitchen. His left arm was bound in a sling.

"Thanks. I thought we'd eat outside since it's not too cold." Jan pushed the door leading to her back porch open with one foot and slipped outside. Her dad followed, with a dish of pencil-thin asparagus in his good hand.

Jan went back into the kitchen and returned with a bottle of ketchup. She squeezed a puddle of it onto her plate and offered the bottle to her dad.

He waved it away. "I can't believe you're going to drown this good food in that stuff. You put it on everything when you were little, but I always thought you'd grow out of it." He put down his fork and squeezed her hand. "Can you try not to tear up every time I say I remember something?"

"Sorry, Dad," Jan said. She took a deep breath and poured some lemonade into their glasses. She was struggling to find her equilibrium in this new world, but she was thrown off balance by even the smallest reminders of the changes in store for her and her dad. No matter how she tried to structure her life, to find a new routine in the midst of this chaos, she knew every month, every day could bring a paradigm-shifting change. The security she had found with her new job and her new home had been disrupted, and she was thrown back to the constant movement she had experienced in childhood. Only this time, she would probably have to face most of it alone.

"Delicious asparagus," her dad said in the upbeat tone he always used when he wanted to cheer her up.

"I found it at the farmers' market, along with the fresh thyme I used on the potatoes."

"You should make this exact meal when we invite your new friend for dinner. What's her name? Tina?"

"Why would I invite her over? We're not dating, Dad."

He only smiled at her outburst. "I didn't say you were. Don't worry, I'm not expecting her to ask for your hand in marriage. But I'd like to meet the woman who's going to be living in my apartment. And I'll bet she'd like a home-cooked meal."

Jan dipped a potato in ketchup and popped it in her mouth. She was not inviting Tina to her house and cooking a meal for her. Tina already seemed to see her as someone frumpy and boring, so serving meatloaf as if she were some sort of fifties' housewife was so *not* going to happen. She wasn't about to admit to her dad that she had been imagining Tina here with them. In her home, sharing a meal, complimenting her cooking. Taking her upstairs to bed after they ate. "I'll see if she wants to meet us for lunch sometime. In a restaurant."

"Ah, I see," her dad said as he served himself another slice of meatloaf. "She must be too pretty to be trusted anywhere near your bedroom."

"She's not…I am not going to have a conversation about women or my bedroom with you."

"Fine, I'll stop teasing." Her dad smiled, but it faded and his expression turned serious. "But I want to see you dating. Falling in love. So I don't have to worry about you being alone."

Jan took a drink of lemonade, letting the tart, icy liquid cool the sudden heat of emotion she felt spreading through her throat and tear-filled eyes. She carefully set her glass down so it evenly matched up with the ring of condensation it had left on the table. She would not let him guilt her into searching for love before she was ready. "I'll date once I have the rest of my life in order."

"Maybe if you let yourself fall in love, you wouldn't mind so much when life doesn't go as planned."

Falling in love would only confuse things more. The idea of having a partner, a constant, in her life had its appeal, but it was fantasy. In her experience, love had been as fleeting as home, school, and friends. "I promise I'll go out more once we're more settled. But believe me, Tina is not what I need right now."

"All right, I'll drop the subject. For now," her dad added. "Did I see a pie on the kitchen counter?"

Jan smiled and gratefully accepted the change in topic. "Strawberry-rhubarb. And ice cream. But you can't have any if you keep discussing my romantic life."

"Like you have one to discuss," he muttered. "That was a joke, darling daughter," he said when she glared at him. "I'll stop now. I'm not going to risk losing dessert privileges."

❖

Tina let her car idle for a moment when she got back to the apartment on Thursday. Jan was sitting on her doorstep, reading a magazine. Another visitor. Already today, her meeting with Peter had gone later than expected because her Uncle Nick had stopped by the nursery to see her. He had caught her in a bear hug so tight and so long lasting, it squeezed the guilt right into her chest, where it now sat like a lump. Tina knew Nick had been very close to his older brother—close enough to name his only son, Peter, after her dad—and she had witnessed his despair at the funeral. But today she had looked at him through an adult's eyes, not a child's. Now she could begin to imagine how difficult it had been for him to not only lose a sibling, but also to lose touch with his brother's family. Like Peter, he had sent cards and occasional gifts to her and her mom, but the distance between them had been too great to overcome. Tina's mom had never felt comfortable with her husband's family, and after he died she'd wanted nothing more to do with them. Tina had naturally followed her example, cringing inside every time she had to accept some financial assistance because it was her only way to make her mom's last months as peaceful as she could. And she had hated the need to rely on them to help with hospice care.

In a moment of weakness, prompted by Nick's struggle to overcome his emotions and the recognition of her part in their rift, she had agreed to go to Peter's upcoming birthday dinner. Doubtless, it would mean another fun reunion with her grandmother, but she was mature enough to be civil for one night. Or too drunk to care what her grandmother said to her. She wasn't sure yet which option she would choose, but alcohol was the early favorite.

And now the sight of Jan waiting for her made her wish she had canceled their appointment. She felt too raw to deal with a vulnerable, sexy woman, but she hadn't thought to bring Jan's number with her, and she'd deleted it from her phone after their first conversation. She was sure Peter had Chloe on speed dial by now, so she could have asked him to relay the message, but she hadn't wanted to tell either of them about her project until she knew whether Jan had told them about her father. So she had no choice but to be polite but distant and get the meeting over quickly.

"Don't you have another key?" she asked as she walked up the path. The apartment was one of four units in a horseshoe-shaped complex. Jan's dad's was in the back, farthest from the street and with a view of the alley behind it. Nothing fancy, but it was quiet and comfortable.

Jan closed her magazine and stood. "Yes, but I didn't want to intrude on your privacy. While you're staying here, it seems like your place."

Tina frowned. Why didn't anyone understand? She didn't belong here, didn't have a place in this city or in their lives. She was just passing through.

"Next time, go inside instead of sitting on the porch," she said as she unlocked the door. Jan looked startled by the roughness in her voice, but she followed Tina inside in silence and shut the door behind them.

"I trust you not to go through my suitcases or steal my underwear," Tina added, trying to turn her outburst into a small joke. It didn't work, so she handed Jan the package in her hands instead.

"Here are the feeders you wanted. Chloe told Peter to give them to me to give to you."

"Thank you," Jan said as she opened the bag and took out a tissue-wrapped package. "I've been meaning to stop by his nursery, and this saves me a trip."

She seemed so relieved that Tina felt a bit sorry for the way she had complained to Peter about her lack of privacy. Maybe she had made a bigger deal about the brief relay of information than had been warranted. Still, her every move seemed monitored by the quickly formed group of friends. She had expected more anonymity in Spokane than she had found.

"Dad's always been interested in birds," Jan continued. "I thought he'd like to see these in the tree outside his window. Oh, this is lovely."

Two of the feeders were standard tube feeders, but the one Jan held was a delicate blown-glass bulb with tiny red perches attached to the bottom.

"Another of Peter's personal favorite things," Tina said, smiling at the memory of him gushing about the local artist's work. "Although I suspect anything made or grown in a twenty-mile radius of Spokane qualifies for the honor. It's for hummingbirds."

"What do I owe you?"

"Nothing. They're a gift from Peter." *Because he's trying to get in your friend's pants.* Tina almost spoke the words out loud, but she had a feeling Peter would have made the same gesture even if he had never met Chloe.

"He's very nice," Jan said, holding the glass feeder so it caught the sunlight streaming through the front window. "You're lucky to have an extended family like you do. I know your relationship might be strained, but still…at least you're all making an effort."

Jan's words echoed the guilt-ridden thoughts Tina had been fighting since seeing Uncle Nick again. But it had been too long, and the issues were too complex. She couldn't just forget the years when her only family, her whole world, had been contained in the small apartment she'd shared with her mother. "I'm here to pad my portfolio and fulfill a family obligation. Not to make amends. Sure, Peter's a nice guy, but once I finish this project I'm out of here."

Jan looked about to say something more, but Tina stopped her. "We should get to work. Where are your dad's photos?"

Jan hesitated, but let the matter drop. "In the bedroom closet."

Tina trailed after her down the short hallway. She understood Jan might be feeling lonely right now, without anyone to share the responsibility of looking after her father, but Tina had been in the same situation once. And she had quietly dealt with it on her own, not asking for help until it was desperately needed. And definitely not prying into anyone else's personal family business. Jan was gorgeous and had flashes of humor and lightness, but Tina's first instincts about her had been correct. Tina's memories were already teasing her with guilt, and she didn't care to add Jan's sanctimonious voice to the mix.

Jan stopped in the doorway. "You haven't unpacked yet. Are you planning to live out of your suitcases for three months?"

Tina had been in the apartment since Monday, but she hadn't been able to make herself unpack. To put her clothes in the dresser and make her decision to stay final. She had hung up a couple of her nicer outfits, but everything else was crammed haphazardly in her bags and stacked in the corner of the room. And she was tired of Jan's preachy ways.

"I'm still not sure how long I'm staying. If I can get through my obligations sooner than expected, I'll go home. Besides," she added with a half smile as she stepped closer to Jan, "I don't want to give any *houseguests* the wrong idea. That I'm here to stay. I'm sure you understand what I'm saying."

Jan felt her cheeks flush, proving she knew exactly what Tina meant. She had a feeling Tina's presence, so close she could feel a slight caress of Tina's breath when she spoke, had as much to do with her blush as her innuendo did. She hadn't imagined Tina bringing dates back to the apartment, but of course, she couldn't expect Tina to remain celibate all summer. The sudden image of Tina in this room with a woman, kissing her as they moved toward the bed, groping blindly past fabric to flesh, hit Jan with such a rush of arousal and frustration she felt weak. She walked quickly to the closet and stepped inside, brushing against a silk blouse of Tina's and catching a trace of the scent she had already come to associate with her. Pine and peach. Not a perfume, but maybe something Tina kept in her closet back home. She pulled a heavy box off the shelf and handed it to Tina before grabbing a second box.

"Kitchen table?" Tina asked and Jan nodded, following her out of the bedroom that was suddenly infused with an imagined musky smell and the sound of climactic gasps and the disturbing vision of Tina, nestled between some stranger's legs.

Tina set the box on the kitchen floor and tidied the small stack of notebooks and loose papers scattered on one end of the table. Jan just watched, in awe at how quickly she could remove any trace of her presence from the kitchen. Tina lived in the corners of the apartment. Her violin case and a music stand were tucked in the corner of the living room, her suitcases in the bedroom, and her work supplies on the table. As if pressing toward the middle of the space would somehow trap her there, removing any chance of escape.

"Is that your new logo for the nursery?" she asked, spotting the green-and-brown sketch before it was whisked away. Tina put the drawing back on the table and unzipped a small plastic pouch. She pulled out a drafting pencil and made a few changes to the logo.

"This was one of my first ideas. The one Peter finally chose will be curved here and here. And the capital letters will look like this."

"Oh, very appealing," Jan said as she leaned over Tina's shoulder to watch her work. She tried to concentrate on the lines flowing from Tina's pencil, not her slender and sure fingers as they moved across the page. "Like an old-fashioned country store."

"Exactly the look I was going for," Tina said as she put the pencil away. "Because the image carries with it all the suggestions of personal service, wide selection, and community feel you'd expect from a store like that."

Tina put the papers on the kitchen counter. "Now I just need to come up with a slogan. Then I can get to web design."

"You're enjoying the work, aren't you?" Jan asked. Tina normally looked so confident and measured, but a restless edge passed over her face when she talked about her work. As if she had a buildup of creative energy and was about to set it free. Jan liked the hint of wildness, of passion, something Tina usually seemed determined to hide as she stood apart from everyone in her cool, detached way.

Tina grinned. "I am, but don't tell Peter. I'm trying to maintain my reputation as the long-suffering, put-upon cousin. I like being in charge of the whole creative process, from concept to application." She went to the fridge and peered inside. "I don't know if you've eaten dinner yet, but I'm starved. All I can offer is cold pizza and beer. Typical bachelor-pad food. Or we can order something if you'd rather."

"Sounds more like college-dorm food," Jan said, settling at the table and pulling a stack of photos out of her box. "And it sounds good to me. How about some music while we do this? I can play one of Dad's old records."

She returned to the living room and hunted through the old LPs until she found the one she wanted. The faded and torn cover showed an old Cajun band, including a fiddle player. She picked it because it was one of her dad's favorites, not because she thought Tina might enjoy it.

"Cool music," Tina said when Jan came back to the kitchen, the slightly scratchy sound of stylus on vinyl following her. "I study all kinds of fiddle styles—just as a hobby—and Cajun is one of my favorites. Great dance music."

"Dad was stationed near Shreveport for about five years, starting when I was four. Just a few years after my mom left. It was the longest we ever stayed in one place until he came here to Fairchild when I was in college. We went on day trips every time he had a day off, and when I think back, those years seem like a long string of county fairs and city tours. Lots of great food and music and horse-drawn carriages. I think he was trying to make up for her not being there."

"Do you keep in touch with her?" Tina asked. Jan had noticed her habit of sitting very still when she listened, as if she was carefully observing and mentally recording everything she heard and saw. Jan avoided eye contact and instead picked at the label on her beer.

"I had lunch with her twice when I was fifteen, a sophomore, because we were in California for six months. She lives in Pasadena, just a half-hour drive from the house we were renting." Jan started with the numerical details because the emotions were too difficult to explain. "She had a new family, and there was just no real connection between us. I couldn't remember much about her, and I sort of felt empty when we talked. I guess I had expected to finally find some sort of home with her, a place where I fit. But she was a stranger. We were polite, but our relationship ended there."

"Weren't you angry? I mean, she abandoned you. You must have been pissed when you finally confronted her."

Jan shook her head. "Just disappointed, I guess. I resented all the moving around. Like something was missing, but every time I thought I might have figured out what it was we had to leave again. I thought she was the answer, but she wasn't. Truthfully? Nowadays, I rarely even think about her." Jan laughed, but it only came out as a dry sound, like a cough. She took a sip of her beer. "I'm not one who should be lecturing you about staying in touch with relatives, am I?"

"Families are complicated," Tina said. "Maybe someday you'll want a chance to get to know each other. When you've found your sense of home and can meet her without any expectations."

"Maybe."

They fell silent, and Jan munched on her pizza as she sorted through the photos. They had been stored with no respect to order or date, and she felt as if she was watching her life flash before her eyes in a decidedly random way. She was sixteen, she was two, she was five. Each picture brought an onrush of surrounding memories, and the haphazard journey through the ages disoriented her. She eventually stopped and concentrated on her beer instead, watching Tina go into work mode as she shuffled through the memorabilia of virtual strangers. She seemed to have some sort of system in place already, and she rapidly sorted her photos into piles, occasionally asking Jan about a person or location.

Tina extracted a couple of pictures from one of her piles. She looked up at Jan with a quizzical expression. "How many pink bedrooms did you have? I've seen at least three."

"All of them," Jan said without hesitating. "They were all pink because it was my favorite color. Dad always painted my room first thing when we moved to a new place, even if we were only staying for a few months." Jan frowned as she tried to mentally count how many different rooms she had lived in while growing up. The familiar color on the walls had made them blend together into a comforting image of one room. "Twelve," she finally said.

"That's a lot of pink paint," Tina observed. "Shh…I like this song." She listened to the faint music, her head cocked to one side and a faraway look in her eyes. Like a wild animal listening to a noise in the distance. When the song ended, Tina went into the living room and Jan followed. Tina seemed to be on some sort of mission, so Jan quietly sat on the couch, waiting to see what happened. Tina switched off the record player, went over to the corner of the room, and opened her fiddle case. Jan gave a small gasp of surprise when she saw the delicate instrument. Just the shape of a violin, the mere idea of one, outlined in bright-red curving wood. Sexy and slender. As if it had been carved just for Tina.

Tina seemed focused on the music in her head, and she quickly plugged the violin into an amplifier and adjusted the settings. She rosined her bow, and something fell into place in Jan's mind. She scooted down the couch and picked up the cake of rosin. She sniffed it. Pine, with a hint of peach.

Tina began to play the song she had just heard. Without music, without fumbling for notes. Jan sat in stunned silence as she listened. She remembered struggling for days to memorize a simple piece for her one-and-only piano recital. Luckily, she had moved soon after, and her nomadic lifestyle had made regular lessons impractical. She had never gotten past playing a few simple songs out of a book, let alone repeating entire pieces after one hearing.

When Tina finished, she smiled almost shyly at Jan as if she had forgotten she wasn't alone.

"How did you do that? Have you heard the song before?"

Tina shrugged, her violin still propped under her chin. "I learned by listening to my grandpa and my parents, and then trying to repeat what they played. By the time my dad died, I could mimic pretty complex pieces, without too many mistakes. I didn't know any other way. The first time I had any formal musical training was in my middle-school orchestra." Tina lowered the violin and frowned. "My teacher thought I was a troublemaker. I couldn't read a note of music, but we played simple songs, all familiar to me. So I'd read the title and play the song, but never just as it was written, of course. My family played fiddle music, so I was accustomed to improvising and embellishing, especially when I was bored by the other students who could barely string two notes together. She kept shouting at me to play the correct notes, but I had no idea what I was doing wrong. The songs sounded right to me."

"Didn't you tell her you couldn't read music?" Jan asked. She heard the edge of frustration in her own voice as she imagined the gifted young musician being cruelly and unfairly criticized.

"I tried, but she didn't believe me because I was playing so much better than the other kids. My mom would have helped me through it, but she had just been diagnosed with lung cancer, and I worried I'd make her sicker if I complained about school. So I stuck it out because it was so important to her that I have music in my life."

Jan moved over as Tina sat next to her on the couch. She held out her hands for the violin and Tina handed it to her. The wood felt smooth and cool to her touch, polished to a glossy finish and fitted with metal levers instead of wooden tuning pegs. Such a modern, restrained instrument, but in Tina's hands it sounded so warm as it brought traditional music to life.

"I promised Mom I'd play in high school as well," Tina continued. "Although I probably would have quit for good after I graduated if I'd had another bad experience. I thought I was muddling through okay, but after a couple weeks, my new orchestra teacher asked me to stay after class. He put a piece of sheet music on my stand, with the title blacked out, and asked me to play it." Tina laughed at the memory. Jan handed the instrument back and watched as Tina ran her hand over the ebony fingerboard. "I had no clue what song it was, so I just sat there. I figured he was going to kick me out of the class. Instead, he asked a few questions about how I had learned to play, and then he calmly started teaching me the names of the notes. What a gift he gave me."

Tina elbowed Jan gently in the side. "I had some teachers who really made a difference in my life, who helped me through when things were so bad at home," she said. "I never would have graduated without them. You have an amazing opportunity to help kids, and from what Chloe said, it sounds like you're doing a great job at it."

"I love what I do," Jan said. Tina watched her twist a lock of hair around her finger as she spoke. The gold of a wheat field, heated by the sun. "I feel I have an opportunity to teach so much more than geometry, although the subject fascinates me and I enjoy sharing it with my students. But I also want to teach them how to solve problems, to think, to enjoy learning. I'll bet you'd be a wonderful music teacher."

Tina picked up her bow and brushed rosin dust off her lap. Anything to keep her from staring at the way Jan's hand sifted through her own hair and made it catch the light. Suddenly restless, she got to her feet and played "Jolie Blon." Because it was one of the first songs she had learned from her grandpa. Not because the pretty blonde on the couch had any effect on her.

"What song is that?"

Tina laid her violin in its case. "I don't remember the title," she lied. "It's just an old Cajun tune." She paused, thinking back to her sophomore year and the decisions she'd made. She had taken classes in education and loved them, but the thought of being a teacher had terrified her. Being responsible for all those kids, like being the head of a big family. They'd have needed her, relied on her, depended on her. She couldn't do it. "You know, I thought about becoming a teacher when I was in college. But I was too anxious to get away from the rules and routine of school to sign up for a lifetime of structure. I can't imagine giving up the freedom to move if I want to and to set my own hours. I like to keep my options open in work…and in other areas of my life," she said, with a casual wink at Jan. "I like variety."

"Must be nice," Jan said briefly. Tina sighed. Good. She had managed to break the moment of connection she had felt with Jan, the moment caused by the weakness of nostalgia, not by any real bond between them.

Jan stood and got her things. "I should be going. Dad will be expecting me."

"Sure. And I think I'll head out to check the nightlife around here. I'll call if I have any questions about the photos."

Jan paused with her hand on the doorknob. "He wants to meet you sometime. I said I'd ask if you want to go to lunch, but if you'd rather not…"

"I'd like to," Tina answered too quickly. "For the project, I mean. It'd be helpful if I got to know him a little before I start piecing his life together."

"Okay. I'll call, and we can set a time. 'Bye."

Tina watched her walk down the path and across the street to her car before she shut the door. She really needed to get out. Put on a sexy outfit and head to the nearest bar. Maybe later. She turned on the phonograph and played along with the music, weaving her own version of the melody around the band's recording.

CHAPTER SEVEN

Peter dragged Tina around the bar on Tuesday night and introduced her to each person in the room, whether they were there to play at the open session or simply to drink and enjoy the music. He seemed to know everyone, but the faces had no meaning to Tina, and she forgot names as quickly as Peter said them. Once she heard people play, learned their individual styles and sounds, she would know them. As she had come to expect, there was no one type of person at the session—male and female, college students and old-timers, all of them there because they loved the music and the traditions they were about to share. Tina followed Peter around the bar with a beer in one hand and her violin case in the other, feeling more relaxed and at home than she had since arriving in Spokane. She occasionally put the drink on a table to shake hands with someone. She tried to focus on the faces in front of her, but half her attention was on the front door.

The only reason she cared about Jan's anticipated arrival with Chloe was because she had a couple of questions about Jan's dad's military career. She had agreed to come to O'Boyle's with Peter because she had spent the weekend working on her two projects and needed a break. The sooner she finished the DVD and Peter's PR work, the sooner she could get back to Seattle where she belonged. Spokane was proving to be a lonely place.

Someone captured Peter's attention for a moment, and Tina took a break from swimming through the crowd of strangers. She knelt near the small square table Peter had claimed for them and checked her amp, making sure her settings were low enough so her violin would blend with the group. She'd be able to adjust the volume as the night wore on and the bar got noisier. After a quiet weekend in the apartment, she was looking forward to the sounds of an open session, the cacophony of varied styles, abilities, and interpretations of the music. Tina loved the chaos because it occasionally produced an unexpected and harmonious magic. And sometimes it was simply loud and fun and surprising. Exactly what she needed tonight.

Tina had planned on having the past weekend to herself. She had decided not to answer the phone when Jan or Peter called, to give herself a break from their demands on her—to be nice to the family, to unpack, to settle in—when all she wanted was to be left in peace, to go her own way. Her defiance wasn't tested, though, since neither one of them tried to contact her. She had called Andy and Brooke to pass the time on Saturday night, but about an hour into their conversation she realized she was being as demanding and needy as the people she was trying to avoid. She had hung up the phone, resolved to get through her projects as quickly as she could. Then she'd be free to return to her life in the city. Anonymous, unfettered, and fun.

"Hi." The single word, spoken in Jan's quiet voice, startled Tina. She rose out of her crouched position and banged her head on the edge of the table.

"Ouch, damn it. Hi yourself." Tina stood up and rubbed her head. She let her hand drop when she saw the drawn look on Jan's face. Dark circles shadowed her eyes, making them look almost navy, and the familiar frown line creased her forehead. "You look like hell. Are you sick?"

"Jesus, what a way to greet someone. I'm still waiting to see the legendary charm Brooke warned me about."

Tina pulled out a chair and waved Jan into it. "Really, what's wrong? Is it your dad?"

Jan's eyes widened slightly as if in surprise. "Well, yes. He's having some complications after his surgery. The doctor was worried it was a blood clot forming, so he's back in the hospital for a few days. I think he was in a lot of pain before he finally told me, but I should have figured it out. He looked feverish this weekend, but he never complained." Jan rubbed the bridge of her nose. "Sorry. I shouldn't have come. I don't think I'm up for a night out."

Tina reached across the table and eased Jan's hand away from her eyes. "Do not feel guilty," she said in a stern voice. "You've been a wonderful daughter. Besides, I found some military papers in the box of pictures," she continued, lightening her tone to try to coax a smile from Jan, "commendations and things about your dad, and he sounds like one tough dude. He probably could have a stake through his heart and say it's just a splinter."

"An exaggeration, but you're right—he isn't a complainer. And he *is* stubborn."

Tina squeezed Jan's hand before she let it go. "Next time, call me if you need any help," she said before she remembered the vow she had made not to answer any of Jan's calls over the weekend. "So, I'm surprised to see an old schoolmarm like yourself out on a Tuesday night. Don't you have class tomorrow?"

"She's such an old fuddy-duddy, she gets her lesson plans written by the first of every month," Chloe said as she joined them. She handed a beer to Jan and set her own on the table. "Unless she has assignments to grade, she has every evening free. Too bad she wastes them by staying in and getting to bed by ten."

"Is she serious?" Tina asked Jan.

"Partially," Jan said, with a scowl in Chloe's direction. "But she doesn't need to make it sound like a character flaw to be prepared."

Chloe ignored her comment. "Peter just showed me his mandolin. It's so beautiful and it feels like satin. I can't wait to hear him play."

"Oh, Peter, your instrument is so big!" Jan said before she took a sip of her beer. Her voice mimicked Chloe's gushing tones exactly.

"May I touch it? Oh, please, may I?" Tina added in a breathy voice.

Jan choked as she struggled to swallow her beer, and then she joined Tina's sexy, throaty laughter. "Oh, don't go, Chloe," Jan said when her friend stood up with a frown.

"There is something seriously wrong with you two," she said before she walked away from the table.

"Do you think we went too far?" Jan asked. This was exactly what she needed tonight. Laughter and teasing. The company of someone light and frivolous. Tina was certainly not a permanent solution to any problem Jan might have, but she was a good source of temporary stress relief. As long as Jan kept herself in check and didn't let things go further than friendly banter. Otherwise, she might end up wanting more.

"I'm sure she'll be fine. I'm just shocked my cousin inspires so much adoration and lust in anyone."

"Really? Don't you realize he looks enough like you to be your twin?" Jan spoke without thinking. Tina stared at her, her bottle raised halfway to her mouth, and Jan was relieved when the evening's session leader stepped up to the mic.

Chloe and Peter, carrying his inlaid and burnished mandolin, returned to the table. She was looking somewhat less angry, but she stuck her tongue out at Jan when she sat down. Jan smiled back and then turned her attention to the stage, trying to ignore the sight of Tina shrugging out of her sweatshirt and straightening the black tank she wore underneath.

"I see some unfamiliar faces in the audience, so let me begin by explaining how we run a session here at O'Boyle's," the gray-haired man said, in a heavy Irish accent. "As evening's host, I'll start us off with some of my favorite tunes. As we go on, feel free to call out requests. And if you don't have an instrument, you're welcome to sing along or keep the rhythm with your hands or feet. Now, I remember when I was a wee lad in Dublin—"

"Try Cincinnati," Peter called out.

"I forgot to mention," the host said, all traces of his brogue gone, "any disruptive elements will be removed at the discretion of the session leader. Now, where was I? Ah yes. When I was a wee lad…"

Jan half listened to his clearly fabricated tale of childhood while she watched Tina rosin her bow in long sweeping strikes. She looked so at home, her pose casual and her hands moving deftly over her instrument as she prepared to play. She was in her element in this place, where musical rules were discarded and identities were created to suit the occasion. Jan knew she shouldn't stare, shouldn't give in to her desire to watch only Tina in the room full of musicians, but she couldn't stop. And once the group started playing a rousing jig, Tina seemed so engrossed in the music, bending her notes around the basic melody, that Jan assumed she was unaware of the attention.

Fortunately. Because Jan didn't want to look anywhere else. She had watched Tina play the refined and elegant quartet music on her acoustic violin at Brooke's rehearsal, but this was something else entirely. Jan was surprised by the sheer physicality of Tina's playing. Caught in the wave of improvisation, Tina's whole body seemed to resonate with her fiery fiddle. The tendons in her neck and the muscles in her arms were taut, but her fingertip touch on the bow was light and flexible. Her right foot and upper body kept time to the music, but her expression was unruffled and serene.

After a few songs, the session leader beckoned at Tina. "Hey, newbie," he said, raising the mic a few inches. "Why don't you turn up the volume and show us what your pretty red beast can do."

Tina stepped up to the stage without hesitating. "Do any of you know 'Mountain Spring'?" A few hands went up. "Great. Join in whenever you want."

Jan watched her take a deep breath before she raised the fiddle. Her eyes drifted closed as she played the first long down-bow of the Celtic tune. After a few measures, other instruments in the group picked up the melody, and at the first sound of other voices joining her own, Tina opened her eyes and smiled. At first, the other players merely echoed the simple phrasing of the song, but gradually, individuals broke off and added their own embellishments. Jan saw a helix in her mind, a curved line spiraling up, adding layers and depth but always twisting around the axis of Tina and her violin. Tina looked at her, as if she felt the weight of Jan's stare, and the rest of the room receded, leaving only Tina as the center of the song.

When the last notes of the song faded away, Tina broke their eye contact and returned to her seat. Jan felt hot, wet. She took a drink of her beer, but it was too warm to do any good.

The host returned to the mic and cleared his throat loudly. "Damn," he said. "I think I need a cigarette after watching you play like that."

"Stop," Tina said with a grin, running her fingers over the violin. "You're making her blush."

Jan joined in the group's laughter, but the sound she made sounded rough and false. She had felt the song as if it was meant only for her, but the man's words helped her return to common sense.

Tina oozed sexuality. Her charisma was natural and affected everyone around her. The intimate way she had played hadn't been intended for Jan. She couldn't let herself be fooled into thinking it had.

❖

Tina numbly played a few more tunes with the group before she excused herself and went into the bathroom. She splashed cold water on her face and leaned against the counter, staring at the mirror. Her high ponytail, meant to keep her hair out of her face while she played, revealed her flushed neck and chest. The small red mark made by her shoulder rest, usually prominent on her pale skin, was barely discernible against the color of her arousal. She still wasn't sure what had happened while she was on the stage. She was accustomed to using music to attract women, to seduce them, but never before had she herself been seduced. Her mind had fabricated a story with Jan in the lead role, and she had simply poured the images into the music she played.

A mountain spring, a lush green meadow, sun heating her back as she braced her arms on either side of Jan's face. Kissing her lips, nuzzling her hair, nipping at her neck and collarbone. The feel of Jan's hands sliding up her back and into her hair. Pushing her lower.

"Oh my God," she said to her reflection. "You need to stop."

She paced back and forth in the small space. Okay, she was obviously attracted to Jan. And, just as obviously, they were not suited to each other in any way except physically. Tina would easily be able to have a few nights of fun before she moved on, went home. But would Jan be able to just have sex without figuring the affair—and Tina—into her life plan? No. She was too serious and alone. Maybe she had been watching Tina as if she was about to pounce on her, but she wouldn't be satisfied with a brief fling. And brief was all Tina was about.

The pep talk worked, and Tina returned to the table with more composure. She needed to avoid Jan until she could find some more appropriate female companionship. Get this out of her system, whatever it was.

The musicians were taking a short break, and Peter and Chloe were settled cozily in a conversation. Tina looked around for something safe to occupy her and Jan.

"Want to play some pool?" she asked. A nice, unromantic game of pool, she added silently.

"Sure," Jan said, following Tina to an empty table at the back of the room. She sorted through the cue sticks, putting more attention on the task than seemed necessary, while Tina expertly racked the balls. "Why don't you break," Jan said.

"Okay." Tina hefted a couple of cues before she found a comfortable one. "But I should warn you, I'm good at any game you can practice in a bar."

"Cocky. Care to back your bragging with a bet?"

Tina's mind ran through several wagering possibilities. Trouble was, she wouldn't care if she won or lost with any of them. "Do you mean money?"

Jan hesitated long enough for Tina to suspect that her thoughts had been roaming in the same direction. "Of course I mean money. Twenty?"

"You're on," Tina said, striking the cue ball with a loud crack. She watched an orange ball drop into a pocket. "Solids."

She sank the seven but missed the next shot. Jan stepped up to the table. "And I should warn you," she said.

"Yeah?" Tina asked, focused more on Jan's ass than her words.

"I doubt I spend nearly as much time as you do in bars, but I happen to know a thing or two about geometry. And pool is all about angles and lines."

She knocked the thirteen ball into the side pocket with a confident whack, followed by a tricky bank shot to drop the fourteen. Tina's attention returned to the game as two more stripes fell in succession.

"And a little physics," Jan added as she put some backspin on the cue ball so it snapped to a halt on the edge of a pocket instead of dropping after the nine. Lining her up for an easy shot on the ten, and then the eleven.

"Eight, corner pocket," she said, pointing with her cue. "Might want to get that twenty out."

Tina stared at her, openmouthed, as she made the shot. Jan was sexy. Jan leaning over a pool table was incredibly sexy. Jan handily winning the game took Tina's breath away.

Peter and Chloe walked over just in time to witness Tina's disgrace as she gave Jan a twenty. "Looks like she trounced you,

Cousin," Peter said. He looked at the table with most of the solid balls still scattered on it. "Did you sink *anything*?"

"Shut up, *Cousin*," Tina said, jabbing him in the ribs with her stick.

"You played a good game," Jan said. "I thought the strategy of leaving all your balls on the table so they got in my way was brilliant."

Tina was tempted to chase Jan around the table, but she wasn't sure she'd be able to control herself once she caught her. "Is the music starting again?" she asked instead.

"In a minute," Peter said. "Some people are going to Coeur d'Alene this Saturday to see a local Irish band play. The Boise Banshees. Chloe and I thought the four of us could go."

Tina stayed quiet, expecting Jan to be the first to back out of anything resembling a double date. "I'm in," Jan said instead. "I'm teaching a seminar for some grad students at U of I in the morning, but I can hang around town until you get there." She shrugged at Tina as if to apologize for accepting the invitation. "Dad won't be home until Monday at the earliest, so I'd rather be out than sitting at home."

"We're leaving after I'm through with work in the afternoon," Peter said. "So we can take you with us, Tina."

"Oh, our first road trip," Chloe said, in the same cooing voice Tina and Jan had mimicked earlier. Tina groaned. She was starting to like her cousin. But her cousin in love was a bit much to take.

"Or you can drive with me," Jan suggested. "We could get lunch or something after my seminar."

"Thank you," Tina said with relief. A few hours with Jan—in the safety of a public place and broad daylight—plus a chance to hear a new band sounded oddly appealing. Only because her previous weekend had been so boring, and she was anxious for a chance to get out of Spokane, even if only for one day. Jan's company was a minor inconvenience, and certainly not the reason Tina said yes.

❖

Jan let herself into the dark, empty house and leaned against the closed door. Her dad had only been with her for a week before he was back in the hospital, but already the place seemed lonelier than it had before he had come. She'd survive the loneliness, though. She always had. And once she had all the pieces of her life in place, she would start the search for someone to share it with. Not before. Not while everything was so topsy-turvy she could barely make it through a single day without a feeling of vertigo.

Too many loose ends. The house was a great investment if she had the time to do the renovations on her long to-do list. If she had to sell in the near future, so she and her dad could move to a better city for his care? Then it was nothing more than a liability, a huge setback in her plan to build a real home. She moved through the house, turning on as few lights as possible while she prepared for bed. She didn't want to see the harsh lines of reality tonight, when the memory of the dimly lit bar and Tina's presence were so clear in her mind. A night or two with Tina would be a pleasant side trip, a break from her fruitless attempts to reach her goals, but how much more lonely would this place feel when Tina inevitably moved on? Tina wasn't looking for anything permanent—and neither was Jan right now—but the thought of touching her and then watching her walk away was too much to bear.

Jan slid between the sheets and let images from the evening replay in her head. It had taken monumental effort to focus on the pool game instead of on Tina, but it had been worth it to see the expression of stunned appreciation on Tina's face after Jan won the game. She hoped she had made it appear effortless, but with Tina standing so close behind her, she'd been afraid she wouldn't even be able to hit the cue ball, much less run the table. All Tina would have had to do was take one step forward while Jan was leaning over to take a shot, and their hips would have been pressed together. Jan felt warmth spread from the point of imagined contact through her whole body. Tina's music drifted through her mind as she slid her hand over her tense stomach muscles. In real life, she couldn't let Tina get any closer, certainly not close enough to touch. But in her fantasies? She could go all the way.

Chapter Eight

A quiet, boring street. Nothing to see. Tina tried to distract herself with work or television, but she kept returning to the window and twitching aside the curtain. She was anxious to get going because she needed a day trip, a chance to get out of Spokane. Jan's company was just incidental. Tina left the apartment, locking the door behind her, as soon as she saw Jan's Prius pull up to the curb. A whole day together. Brooke would be thrilled, but Tina sure as hell wasn't going to tell her about the outing. She felt safe assuming Jan wouldn't, either.

"Nice car," she said when she sat down. Her car might be a Toyota as well, but the similarity ended there. Jan's was only a year or two old, and clean inside and out. No trails of sticky dried Coke streaking down the dash, or piles of sheet music, art supplies, and fast-food bags littering the backseat. And probably no emergency stash of napkins from McDonald's and cardboard cup sleeves from Starbucks in the glove compartment. There were, however, two large Starbucks coffees in the cup holders.

"Thanks," Jan said as she merged onto the street. She pointed at the coffee. "I hope you like sweet. Mocha on the left, vanilla latte on the right. You get your pick."

Tina took the mocha and moved the latte to the holder on Jan's side. She settled back in her seat and took a sip of her drink. Drops of rain freckled the window as Jan turned toward I-90.

"How far are we going?"

"About a half hour," Jan said. "Coeur d'Alene is just over the Idaho border. It's an easy trip, and there are some beautiful places to hike and camp around the lake. I used to go there a lot with Dad, and with friends when I was in college, but I haven't been for a couple years. How's your PR work for Peter going?"

"Not bad. The drapes for his home-and-garden show booth were the wrong color, so I had to spend a few hours begging and threatening before the company agreed to redo them. And I've been trying to convince Peter to set up a permanent booth at the farmers' market, so he can sell herbs and vegetable starts there. And maybe some of the handcrafted things he loves so much."

"What a great way to connect with the community," Jan said.

"Exactly what I told him. How was your week at school?" Tina asked when it was her turn. She and Jan sounded like they had spent the evening before coming up with safe conversation starters. She hoped they wouldn't be talking about the weather by the time the ride was over. It was supposed to be rainy all day, so the topic wouldn't get them through many miles of drive time.

Tina listened to Jan's stories about her students and was surprised to find she was interested in the unique projects Jan had devised to teach them about geometry and how it applied to architecture. She had really only asked to be polite, but she liked hearing how Jan tried to reach each student as an individual, to understand their struggles and triumphs. Tina knew firsthand from her orchestra experiences the difference a teacher like Jan could make.

She felt strangely comfortable with Jan today, quite a change from their first tension-filled meetings. She was accustomed to forming quick connections with women, but those relationships tended to be fairly shallow. Half an hour of sex was fine—or at least a good start—but the same amount of time stuck in a car with nothing to do but talk? Tina could only come up with a handful of people with whom she'd willingly take a long, sexual-agenda-less drive.

She attributed much of her newfound easy rapport with Jan to her research for the DVD project. The boxes in Jan's dad's apartment were stuffed with documents and pictures, giving Tina an intimate look at Jan's whole life, from babyhood to graduation. Shuffling through the large stack of orders to report to various air force bases had given Tina a more concrete sense of the itinerant life Jan had spent as a child. And there were plenty of photos of Jan standing next to animals, taken in zoos or next to horse-drawn carriages or at fairs, but none of her with a pet of her own. A dog or cat would have been a logistic impossibility for such a mobile family.

Tina had laid out all the pictures of Jan's birthday parties, in chronological order. Jan, her dad, and two or three friends. A pink-frosted cake in front of them on the kitchen table. But the kitchen was different in each one, and so were the friends. She could understand why Jan wanted to find some stability after growing up like she had, but Tina wanted the opposite for herself. While Jan had been traveling the world during high school, Tina had been traveling between home and hospital. She would never regret the time she'd spent with her mom, but she no longer had any deep attachments to another person, and she planned to take full advantage of her freedom.

"I have a question about your dad's career," she said when the conversation about school ended.

Jan flipped the windshield wipers to a higher setting as the drizzle turned to a heavier rain. "Sure, what is it?"

"I don't know much about airplanes, but I've noticed that all of the prints on the apartment walls are of a fighter, but all the pictures of your dad in uniform show him next to a bigger plane. What did he fly?"

"He was a KC-135 pilot," Jan said, with the easy familiarity of someone who had grown up with military designations. "But he always had a thing for the F-15."

"Okay, it's all clear to me now," Tina said sarcastically.

Jan laughed. "The 15 is a small fighter jet, the one in all the prints he's collected. The 135 is a large tanker. So fighter pilots can refuel midair and don't have to land when their tanks are low."

"Like a flying gas station?" Tina asked. Jan nodded. "Sounds dangerous."

"It is, even though Dad always joked that he just had to fly in a straight line, and the fighter pilots behind him were the ones who had to do the real tricky flying. He had a lot of respect for them."

"But he flew fighters before the tanker, didn't he? I couldn't find any photos of him doing that."

"No," Jan said with a slight frown. "I'd have remembered him telling me about that. He started flying 135s the year I was born."

Tina's frown matched Jan's. She'd have to go back through the papers because she must have read them wrong. She moved to the next topic on her list. "So, tell me about this seminar you're teaching."

❖

If the weather had been more cooperative, Tina would have sat outside and read while Jan taught her two-hour seminar. But beautiful as the University of Idaho campus was, Tina didn't feel like sitting in the rain with a soggy book. She had no interest in learning how to teach math to high school students either, but at least the auditorium was warm and dry. She had expected a small room and a handful of graduate students, not tiers filled with over a hundred people. She chose a corner seat and started to read as soon as Jan started to talk.

For about ten minutes, she alternated between pretending to read and actually listening to Jan's lecture. Then she closed her book and concentrated on the completely transformed woman at the front of the classroom. Jan's voice was clear and authoritative, where before it had been conversational. Her whole demeanor reflected the same confidence. Not just her words, but her body language and expression revealed her love of teaching, her belief in the importance of her job. She leaned toward the class, open and relaxed, slowing the pace of her lecture when she came to points she obviously felt were important, taking her time to explain them, as if sharing the knowledge she had was something special and vital. Tina had seen hints of the professional side of Jan in their earlier conversations, but she seemed to belong in front of a class.

Tina just watched at first, mesmerized by Jan's conviction and passion. There was nothing stuffy or boring about her, and Tina felt such a strong attraction she decided she must have a latent teacher fetish. It had to be a general interest in teachers and not a particular interest in Jan that was capturing her attention. Eventually, Jan's words started to penetrate her consciousness, reaching beyond her libido to her brain.

"We can't simply offer our students chunks of knowledge," Jan said, pacing back and forth and gesturing, as if to emphasize the importance of her words, "learned in isolation and discarded after the final exam. We need to connect each lesson to the whole subject and then draw lines from there to the rest of the world. To art and music and sports and literature. Geometry is everywhere, and it's up to us to open our students' eyes to the shape of their universe."

Riffs on a theme. The same thing Tina tried to do with her music. Take a simple melody and make changes to connect it to other genres, to emotions, to life. To her own life. And it was also what she was doing in her PR work for Peter's nursery. Finding a general theme and applying it to all aspects of a company's image. Jan started talking about how she organized her lesson plans, and Tina's thoughts continued to flow. She could tweak Jan's organizational methods and use them to present her business proposals. Take her own fluid ideas and give them shapes. Pyramids, squares, circles, spirals. Whichever best fit the business model of each potential client.

Tina desperately looked around for something to use to take notes. She leaned forward and tapped one of the grad students on the shoulder. "Hey, can I borrow a pen?" she asked when the girl turned around. "And paper," she added.

"Anything else you need?" the student asked in a suggestive voice as she handed Tina a pen and a piece of paper ripped from her notebook.

"This'll do for now," Tina said. She wanted to capture her ideas before they faded away, but old habits made her stop long enough to smile at her benefactor. "But I'll let you know if anything else comes up."

"Then you might need this." The student wrote a phone number on the torn paper on Tina's desk.

Jan cleared her throat, and Tina realized she had stopped lecturing and was watching the exchange. She sketched a wave of apology in Jan's direction before she turned her focus to pouring the inspiration for her newborn business plan onto the page in front of her. She wrote in tiny print, not daring to irritate Jan further by asking for more paper, and by the time the session was over, she had filled both sides with notes.

She waited while the class filed out and Jan collected her supplies. "Great lecture," she said when Jan finally came up the stairs toward her. "You're a very stimulating speaker."

"I didn't think you noticed," Jan said. Her carefully modulated professional voice had disappeared, and her tone held an edge of anger. "You seemed too busy flirting."

"I needed a pen to take notes."

"Because you're planning to be a geometry teacher?"

"No. Because your method for creating lesson plans got me thinking about my business," Tina said, her voice sharp, echoing in the empty room. She had figured Jan would be happy to hear she had inspired Tina with her lecture, but Tina had planned to share her news with Jan in a friendlier, more grateful way. Not by yelling it at her. Jan had been the one to spoil the mood, not Tina.

"Oh, I see." Jan tapped at the paper full of notes. "And this phone number with a heart around it? I suppose you were doing some networking for your *business*?"

"Hey, she was flirting with me," Tina said. She was standing too close to Jan and speaking too loudly. This wasn't personal. Jan was simply angry because Tina had been talking during her class. She took a deep breath but didn't move away. She felt the tension between them as almost a physical connection. An arousing connection. She lowered her voice. "But I didn't discourage it. Sorry."

Jan waved her hand. "Chat with all the pretty grad students you want, just don't do it on my time. If you were in my class I would…" Her voice faltered, and Tina only had to take a small step to move into Jan's personal space.

"You would…what? Have to discipline me?"

Jan laughed and pushed Tina gently in the chest, forcing her to take a step back and breaking the thread of electricity between them. "You can turn off the charm now. I'm the only one here."

"*We're* the only ones here," Tina corrected, gesturing around the room. "And I deserve at least a spanking after talking in class."

"Somehow, I doubt you'd consider it punishment," Jan said. She cleared her throat and stepped away, her attention focused beyond Tina's shoulder.

"Excuse me, but what was the name of the art book you recommended?" One of the grad students was standing by the door. Jan went over to talk to him, and Tina busied herself by folding her page of notes into a tiny square and putting it in her back pocket. She flirted and spoke in innuendo out of habit, but usually it was only a game. Every time her conversations with Jan carried a double meaning, she couldn't seem to erase the resulting visuals from her thoughts. She was trying to decide whether she'd want to be teacher's pet or class troublemaker—or both—when Jan interrupted her dangerous musings.

"What do you want to do now? There are restaurants and lots of shops in town. And I know a couple of places to get awesome cupcakes. We could try one of those."

"Definitely both," Tina decided. "I mean, both cupcake places. We should do a taste test."

"Sounds good to me," Jan said, leading the way out of the classroom.

"To me, too," Tina said quietly. In fact, it sounded much too good.

❖

Jan suggested they take their boxes of cupcakes to the marina. The rain had eased up, turning to a gentle mist, and she desperately needed to be outside in the fresh air. The anger she'd felt when she saw Tina chatting up the grad student had nothing to do with her rules against disruptive talking in class. She had felt a fiery possessiveness, unexpected and unacceptable. And when Tina gave her such a sexy smile and asked to be disciplined? All of Jan's energy—her possessive anger and frustration—had turned immediately to lust. Inappropriately and completely. She clearly was attracted to Tina, a fact proven by repeated fantasies. Hell, she was beginning to accept her inevitable surrender if Tina ever made even a halfhearted attempt to seduce her. But any relationship between them would be fleeting, temporary. And, of course, Tina would run for the nearest escape route at any sign of affection beyond the physical. Leaving Jan heartbroken unless she could get control of her feelings.

Tina opened one of the boxes as they walked. Jan watched her take a huge bite of a red-velvet cupcake before she handed the other half to Jan and licked cream cheese off her fingers. Oh, to be a cupcake. She had a feeling Tina would approach sex the same way she devoured the treats, the same way she played her fiddle. Wholeheartedly and with gusto. Jan wanted to be devoured. To be played like a fine instrument. But Tina's appetites, except for music, appeared to be short-lived. Maybe a dip in the frigid lake would help her cool off. Instead, Jan sat on one of the tall blue stools arranged around a snack bar, still boarded up for the season. She wiped the table with her sleeve so there was a dry place for the pastry boxes.

"You're going to have wet jeans," Tina said. She made a funny coughing sound and sat on the stool opposite Jan. "Well, I guess it doesn't matter."

"I'm sure they'll dry off. Eventually," Jan said. She laughed when Tina looked at her with a quizzical expression, as if she wasn't quite sure what meaning to take from the words. Jan pushed one of the boxes toward her. "Eat," she demanded.

"Gladly," Tina said with a smile. "Where's the peanut-butter one?"

"Here," Jan handed it over and chose a raspberry-and-vanilla cupcake for herself. She moaned in delight as she bit into it, fending off Tina's attempts to take it from her before she finally gave in and traded for the half-eaten peanut-butter and chocolate treat. Fun. She had to acknowledge how much fun she had with Tina. But only because she offered a change of pace, a short and pleasant break from harsh reality.

Jan forced herself to focus on the differences between them, and they weren't hard to find, even in such a silly context. Out of habit, Jan tried to organize the picnic, coming up with an elaborate rating system for their taste test and methodically working through each flavor. Tina refused to play by her rules, though, and her favorite cupcake always seemed to be the one she was eating at the moment.

"I think I'm going to be sick," Jan said after they had finished off the last rich cupcake. "Didn't we buy six so we'd have a couple to take home?"

Tina reached over and brushed her finger against the side of Jan's mouth. Jan sat perfectly still, not even breathing, as Tina licked her finger. "Marshmallow," Tina said. "That one was my favorite."

"Let's walk," Jan suggested, gesturing at the U-shaped boardwalk. Without waiting for an answer, she got up and tossed their trash in a garbage can before she set off at a brisk pace. Damn. One gentle touch and she wanted to devour Tina like one of the sweets. Tina trotted to catch up to her, and Jan launched into a monologue about the lake, the world's longest boardwalk, the natural history of the area, and a description of her favorite local hiking trails. She sounded like an overly enthusiastic tour guide, but she didn't care. She had to keep her mind off sex, and off the nearly irresistible desire she'd had to suck Tina's finger into her mouth.

The water was calm in the marina, painted with the reflections of boats and bright blue awnings. Jan, running out of words before they ran out of boardwalk, stared out toward the lake, where small waves lapped against the floating footpath. "There's a grebe," she said, barely making out the silhouette of the bird rocking gently on the waves.

"Where?" Tina asked, squinting in the direction Jan indicated.

Jan stepped behind her and put her arm over Tina's shoulder, pointing so her finger was directly in Tina's line of sight. She realized she had rested her free hand on Tina's hip, and she had started to shift away when Tina grabbed her wrist.

"Don't move," Tina said. She eased back until her body came in contact with Jan's. Jan couldn't move, didn't want to move. She inhaled the citrusy aroma of Tina's hair, like satin against her cheek. The feel of her breasts pressed against Tina's back, legs and hips joined. Tina slid her hand along Jan's and intertwined their fingers.

Jan dropped the arm she had used to point out the bird and wrapped it around Tina's middle. She felt Tina's sigh, felt her lean into the hug. So quiet. Too quiet. After the morning full of sexual tension, Jan wouldn't have been surprised to feel a desire to kiss Tina, rip her clothes off, make love to her right there on the boardwalk. She had been anticipating such a reaction and was fully prepared to suppress it. But this gentle intimacy, the almost-chaste touch, was too unexpected, too intense. The turmoil that had lately taken up residence in Jan's stomach settled under Tina's touch. And *settled* wasn't a word she should be using in relation to Tina. She stepped away so suddenly Tina stumbled back a couple of steps before she righted herself.

"Hey, what's wrong?" Tina asked, moving toward Jan.

Jan gestured between them. "*This* is wrong."

"Oh my God, we actually touched each other," Tina said in a tone of mock horror. "I'm sure your reputation is tarnished beyond repair."

Jan crossed her arms over her chest. "Don't act like I'm some sort of prude. I just think we should avoid any physical contact." Jan winced. Okay, she sounded like a prude.

"Lighten up," Tina said, with a brief shrug. "So two friends hugged each other. What's the big deal? Besides, you started it."

"And you didn't discourage it," Jan said, echoing Tina's earlier statement. "Must be nice to have women throwing themselves at you constantly."

"You won't hear me complain about it."

"Well, I've never been one to follow the crowd, so why don't you just move on to your next conquest," Jan said before she turned and walked away.

Tina ran her hands through her hair in frustration as she watched Jan leave. Frustration, because Jan was obviously overreacting to a simple hug. And because her own body was betraying her by doing the exact same thing. Tina hadn't felt anything more than the contours of Jan's body pressed against hers and the weight of Jan's arm where it draped around her waist. Nothing overtly sexual, but Tina was wet, her nipples were hard and aching, her breath was short. Hands still, layers of clothes between them, no kissing. She had no reason to feel so exposed and vulnerable.

Tina slowly started walking along the boardwalk after Jan. She had to ease the tension between them, but first she needed to get her self-control in place. She had never reacted to another woman's touch that way. She had sex, she had orgasms, she took control, sometimes she bit. But she *never* melted against a woman like she had with Jan. Never sank into an embrace, without feeling a claustrophobic need for space. Even knowing how different she and Jan were didn't help. Jan's life was bound up in place, family, work. Her future was filled with obligations and plans and structure. Tina wanted freedom and variety. Or, at least, she usually wanted those things, when her hormones weren't in overdrive. She either needed to have sex with

Jan and get her out of her system or find another woman to do the job. The second choice definitely seemed safer.

Above all, she needed to lighten the mood. If she and Jan were angry and hurt, then it meant feelings were getting too serious. When they were teasing and laughing, the feelings remained shallow enough to handle.

She jogged a few steps and bumped into Jan playfully, draping a casual arm across her shoulder. "Hey, I want to thank you."

Jan walked in silence for a few steps, her body stiff, as if determined not to take Tina's bait. "For what?" she finally asked.

"For teaching me a great new pickup line. Hey baby, let me show you this cool bird," she said in the same voice she had used when they were teasing Chloe. "I'll bet you didn't even see a...what did you call it?"

"A grebe, and I did so see one," Jan said in a haughty voice, but Tina saw the corner of her mouth curve into one of her sexy half smiles.

"Ha. Never heard of it. You probably made it up. Anyway, I'm going to join an Audubon group so I can try it out."

"Look," Jan said suddenly, breaking away from Tina's hold and moving to the edge of the boardwalk. Tina came up next to her and peered into the water.

"What now? I don't see...Hey!" Tina shrieked as Jan grabbed her around the waist and pulled her close to the low rope railing.

"I saw a really cool fish. Let me show you," Jan said, tugging Tina precariously close to the water.

"If you throw me in this lake, I'll..." Tina couldn't think of a sufficiently frightening end to her threat. She twisted in Jan's arms and managed to tickle her until she let go. She and Jan backed away from each other, laughing and gasping for air.

"You can try that line at the aquarium," Jan said. She feinted at Tina and laughed harder when Tina playfully batted her away.

Tina sighed in relief as they settled into step next to each other. The angry tension between them seemed to have faded, though Tina's body still felt oversensitive to Jan's nearness. Even the friction of her shirt and jeans as she moved was enough to keep her tight with desire. She wanted Jan's touch. Wanted release. Just...*wanted.* But it was only a conditioned response to the closeness of a beautiful woman. A reflex, nothing more. They still had an hour before they were due to meet Chloe and Peter, so Tina suggested they go to an Irish specialty shop she had noticed near one of the cupcake bakeries.

"I need another fisherman knit sweater," she told Jan as they entered the store. An Irish reel was playing softly over the sound system, and a tower of shamrock-dotted teapots was on display in the front of the store. "My old one is almost worn out."

"I've seen it," Jan said with a grimace. "And I'll be very happy to help you pick out a new one. I accept it as my civic duty to keep you from wearing that beige thing in public ever again."

Tina was about to defend her comfortable old sweater when she noticed a set of prints on the wall. "Ogham writing," she said, aiming toward them. She nodded in response to the clerk's greeting as she walked by the counter.

"What did you call these?"

"Ogham," Tina repeated, spelling the word. "It's an ancient Irish script. It's linear."

"I love the shapes," Jan said, tracing the lines and hash marks without touching her finger to the glass. "It says it means family."

"Ugh," Tina said. Each letter was made up of a vertical line and differentiated by the way one or more horizontal or diagonal lines intersected it. The artist had drawn the letters of each word so they were connected on the vertical, like a tree. Most of the letters in the word for family branched off to the right. Unbalanced. Tina pointed at a different print, with a less lopsided look and more bold diagonal slashes. "I prefer this one. *Laughter.*"

"You know, you could put it up in the apartment. In place of one of the airplane prints."

The one in the bedroom, Tina decided immediately. She pictured the new print hanging there, over the bed, promising laughter and play and connection. "I really don't need to redecorate the place," she said, turning away from the artwork. "It's not like I'll be staying long."

Tina wandered over to the sweaters, oddly disturbed by the exchange. Now she wouldn't be able to be in the bedroom without imagining the print on the wall and remembering their shared laughter on the boardwalk. As it was, Jan had been spending way too much time in Tina's imagination. Like, every night when she was in bed. She hadn't been able even to consider bringing another woman back to the apartment until she could get Jan off her mind. Three was a crowd, in her opinion. She sifted roughly through the clothes on the rack.

"This one," Jan suggested, reaching around her to pull out a heather-green sweater. "It'll be beautiful with your eyes."

She held the sweater against Tina's body to check the size, standing close with her hands on Tina's shoulders. "Not your type?" Jan asked.

"What?" Tina's voice sounded husky and she cleared her throat. "It's fine. I like it."

"Not the sweater," Jan said. "I meant the clerk. She's been staring at you since we came in, and you haven't even flirted with her."

Tina was shocked she hadn't noticed. She couldn't even picture the woman in her mind. Dark blond hair and denim-blue eyes? No. When had Jan managed to superimpose herself over every woman Tina met? She normally could give a damned good description of each woman in a room after a quick scan, but suddenly, she couldn't bring anyone to mind but Jan. "I didn't want to make you mad again. Every time I've flirted today, with you or anyone else, you've snapped at me."

Jan shrugged. "You said it was a habit. Don't fight it on my account."

Tina shrugged back at her. "If you insist," she said, snatching the sweater out of Jan's hands and carrying it to the counter. She was angry. Angry because Jan was complicating what should have been a relaxing evening with friends. And, even more, because she would normally have taken any opportunity to flirt or seduce, but she seemed to be acting decidedly *abnormal* after spending so much time with Jan.

"Did you find everything all right?" the clerk asked.

"Almost. But I haven't learned your name yet," Tina said. Jan made a sound somewhere between a cough and a laugh. Tina ignored her.

"Kris, with a *K*," the clerk said. Her dark brown hair was in a braid halfway down her back, and her eyes were a similar shade.

"Hi, Kris, I'm Tina. You've got great music playing in the store. What group is it?"

"The Boise Banshees," Kris said, gold bangles jingling on her wrist as she held up the CD case for Tina. "They're playing tonight at a bar down the street, if you'll still be in town."

"In fact, they're the reason I came to Coeur d'Alene in the first place," Tina said as she ran a finger over the gold bracelets on Kris's wrist. "At least they *were* the reason I came. Nice bracelets."

"Thanks," Kris said, in a voice sufficiently breathy to let Tina know she had captured her attention. Not that Tina had wanted it in the first place. "I guess I'll see you tonight."

"I'm looking forward to it," Tina said as she picked up the bag containing her new sweater.

"Masterful," Jan said once they were outside.

"Look," Tina said, unaccountably irritable. She felt somehow trapped by her own reputation. She needed women to understand she wasn't looking for anything serious, that she liked playing the field, and she had to act the part, at least around Jan. To do anything less would have made her seem too content just to be with Jan. She wasn't, of course, but she was only here for the music. "All I want to do is listen to this band, not—"

"Hey, there's Peter and Chloe," Jan said, pointing down the street. She headed toward the couple but stopped partway and pulled out her vibrating cell phone.

"It's my dad," Jan said as Peter and Chloe joined them.

Tina reached out and put her hand on Jan's shoulder, all anger about the store-clerk incident dissipating. "What happened? Is he okay?"

"He's fine," Jan said with a frown. "But I need to go back to Spokane."

"I'm going with you," Tina said.

"We'll all go," Peter offered.

"No, please," Jan said, pulling away from Tina's touch. "You go see the band play. It's nothing serious. Sometimes you just need to be with family."

"At least text me when you get home," Chloe said, her concern clearly evident on her face.

"I will. I promise. Have fun tonight."

Tina felt like the last sentence was directed at her. Fun. Right. The day with Jan had been fun, but the night promised to be exhausting. She'd have to endure being a third wheel with the loving couple and discourage Kris's attentions. But she wouldn't add to Jan's distress by making her feel guilty. "I'm sure we will," she said. "Drive safely."

❖

Jan waited until she had turned a corner and was out of sight of her friends before she speed-dialed.

"Hey, Dad, I got your message. No, it's no problem at all," she leaned against a brick building and closed her eyes. "No need to wait until tomorrow. I'm tired from teaching today, so I'm coming back to Spokane a little early and I can bring it by tonight. What kind of cupcake did you want?"

She ended the call and walked quickly to the bakery. She knew she must look as guilty as she felt, glancing around as if she were about to commit a crime. Guilty for being slightly untruthful to her friends. And for using her dad as an excuse to get away from them. But no way could she spend the evening watching Tina seal the seduction deal with her new girlfriend. She was jealous. Illogically and annoyingly jealous. Even though she was attracted to Tina, she didn't want a relationship with her. But the thought of her with another woman made her cringe. And *watching* the seduction process was not an option, so she had to leave. By the time she saw Tina again—even if it was as soon as tomorrow—the relationship probably would have run its course.

To be fair, Tina hadn't seemed at all interested in the clerk until Jan had goaded her into flirting. Jan wasn't even sure why she had been so adamant about pushing Tina. Maybe because she'd felt a physical pain when she had let go of Tina on the pier, and she wasn't convinced she'd be able to make it through the night without throwing her common sense away and throwing herself at Tina. So she had insisted even though Tina had seemed reluctant. But, once Tina had turned on the charm, she took no prisoners. Or maybe one prisoner. Who was about to be tied to Tina's bedposts for the night. Damn.

Jan bought a box of cupcakes and walked back to her car. Three for her dad, and a couple for her on the drive home. Hopefully the sugar rush would distract her enough so she'd stop imagining the inevitable end to Tina's night.

CHAPTER NINE

Tina walked through the empty hallway to Jan's classroom. The door was closed, but it had a small window in it and she peered through. She expected to see students sitting quietly at their desks, most of them nodding off to sleep over their textbooks, while Jan lectured about…Tina struggled to remember her high-school geometry class. Triangles and the Pythagorean Theorem and polygons. Pi.

Instead she saw what looked like a day-care center. The desks had been pushed back against the walls, and all the students were sitting on the floor playing with toy trucks and cars. Jan was on her hands and knees with them, wearing a red T-shirt and black jeans. Snug black jeans. Tina stared at the inch of pale skin showing between Jan's shirt and her jeans. She struggled to swallow her surge of arousal, to banish the memory of Jan's body pressed against her on the pier. She forced her attention off Jan's ass and focused, instead, on her face. A few strands of deep gold hair had escaped her ponytail and curled softly against her cheeks. She looked as young as her students as she pushed her truck over a bridge and laughed along with the kids at some comment Tina couldn't hear.

Tina tapped on the window, and the entire class turned to look her way. Jan's laughter faded to a quizzical expression as she got to her feet.

"What are you doing here?" she asked as she edged out the door and left it slightly open behind her. The abruptness of her question was softened by a smile, and Tina reached over to tuck a loose lock of Jan's hair behind her ear. She needed some contact. Any contact. Or she'd go crazy.

"I was worried about you…about your dad," she said. "I'm meeting Peter here after his lunch with Chloe, and I wanted to check in with you."

"Oh, thank you," Jan said, not looking directly at Tina. "Dad's fine. He's coming back home on Thursday."

"I'm glad," Tina said. She leaned a hand against the wall next to Jan, standing close enough to smell a hint of lavender but not close enough to be able to tell if it was from Jan's hair or her clothes. She wanted to find out. "Too bad you couldn't stay Saturday night. You would have loved the band. And, thanks to you, I had to sit in the backseat of the car and watch the two lovebirds cooing at each other all the way home."

"I thought you'd end up spending the night in Coeur d'Alene."

"No reason to," Tina said. She didn't elaborate. She could easily have found a place to stay for the night, either with Kris or one of the other women who had shown interest, but she had decided to come straight back to Spokane. Even though Jan had left their little party, Tina had still felt her presence. Watching. Judging? Tina hadn't wanted to seduce another woman and take care of her own needs while Jan was alone and scared, taking care of her dad. "So, does your school principal care if you spend class time playing with toys?"

"We're not playing," Jan said, glancing through the window at her students. "The kids built bridges, and we're testing them to find out which designs are strongest. And, yes, they're learning practical applications of geometry and having fun at the same time."

"My teachers weren't as cool as you," Tina said, moving a little closer. The lavender was in her hair. Intoxicating. "Or nearly as pretty."

Jan felt a wave of guilt. It had been building, a tight knot in her stomach, and Jan had thought she could hold it there. Ignore it. Let it sit with the rest of her worries. But Tina was being so nice, so concerned about her. Standing so close and smelling so good. The knot loosened, and the guilt flowed through her and out her mouth. "I lied," she said abruptly.

Tina laughed. "You mean they're not really learning practical applications of geometry?"

"No, I mean yes, they are. But Dad's message on Saturday just asked me to bring him something from the bakery. There wasn't anything really wrong."

"Huh," Tina said, her expression suddenly unreadable. "Why?"

"Because he has a sweet tooth." Jan made a lame attempt at a joke. It didn't work. She wanted to tell Tina the real reason she had left, but she couldn't. Her need to confess had once more come under control. Self-protection was in charge again. "I was tired, and I didn't feel up to a long night in a noisy bar. I didn't want to spoil the evening for the rest of you, so I made an excuse to go home."

"I see. Well, you missed a fun evening."

"I know," Jan said. And she had paid for her fib as she spent the drive home fighting an irrationally superstitious fear that her dad actually would have something wrong with him. But he had been cheerful during her visit, and happy to have the only two cupcakes that had survived her fretful trip.

"I'd better go find Peter," Tina said, backing up a step. "I am glad to hear your dad's okay."

"He still wants to meet you," Jan said as Tina turned to go. "We'd talked about having lunch together, if you still want to...Maybe this weekend?"

"Sure. Give me a call," Tina said over her shoulder as she walked away. She was halfway down the long corridor before she heard the sound of Jan closing her classroom door. Jan's tangled mess of excuses about why she hadn't stayed added up to one conclusion in Tina's mind. Jan was jealous. Her mood had definitely changed while they were in the Irish shop, before the phone message from her dad. Jan might not realize it, and she'd probably never admit it, but she hadn't wanted to stay and watch Tina flirt more with Kris or anyone else. Tina waited for her expected reactions. Panic and claustrophobia because Jan might be developing feelings for her. Or maybe a need to run, an urge to flee because their black-and-white friendship might turn a messy shade of gray. Or maybe, just maybe, she didn't mind at all.

❖

Tina dumped three tiny containers of creamer into her watered-down coffee and stirred while she looked around the diner. The restaurant at Felts Field was one big, chaotic collection of airplane memorabilia. Tina decided it must have been decorated as much by the owners and patrons—given the signed prints, personal photos, and license plates and postcards from around the country—as by a professional designer. The effect was of one enormous collage, even down to the navigational charts and World War II-issue playing cards scattered on her table and covered by a protective sheet of glass. Tina was glad she had arrived early, giving her time to absorb the barrage of images coming from every corner of the room.

Jan had picked the restaurant, located at one of Spokane's smaller airports, because it was one of her dad's favorites. Tina had opted for breakfast because she loved early morning diner fare, with its bad coffee and greasy food. The idea of a family meal, even with someone else's family, usually would have her stomach in knots, but today felt different. Maybe, like Tina's increasing comfort around Jan, it was partly due to her work on the video project. She had been piecing together this man's past through a random collection of photos. She hoped a meeting with him, a chance to talk and ask questions, would help her find the theme she needed to make a cohesive life story. And she had to admit to an interest in seeing Jan interact with her dad. His choices in the past had helped form the woman she was today. And her future was tied to him in ways Jan couldn't yet anticipate. Tina felt an objective curiosity and nothing more. Their future wouldn't affect her in any way.

She watched them come through the door, engrossed in a conversation and seemingly barely aware of their surroundings. Tina had noticed little resemblance between father and daughter in the photos, but she could easily see the similarities in expression and gesture as they talked.

"It was a Cessna 172," Jan's dad said as he stopped by the booth and turned his attention to Tina. "You must be Tina. I'm Glen. No, don't get up. It's nice to finally meet you."

"Hi, Tina," Jan said briefly. "A high-wing? No way. I distinctly remember it was a Piper Cherokee."

"Sit down, daughter. Your mule ears are scraping the ceiling."

"We'll talk about this later," Jan said, scooting into the booth next to him. She started fussing with the table settings, moving napkins and flatware so they were near her dad's good arm.

"I think I'm in trouble," Glen said in a conspiratorial whisper as he leaned toward Tina.

"I think you're right," she whispered back. "I heard the same tone in her voice when she caught me talking during her seminar."

"No one's in trouble," Jan said, moving her dad's water glass closer to him. "You're wrong but not in trouble."

Glen captured Jan's hand as she was reaching for his coffee cup. "If you tuck a napkin in my collar next, I'm upending my hot coffee in your lap."

Tina wrapped both hands around her coffee mug as she watched the two interact, their affection for one another easy to see. But maybe because she was getting to know Jan better, or because she simply was aware of Glen's condition, Tina could see the subtext playing out behind the teasing argument. They were both scared and uncertain but devoted to each other.

"I don't know much about airplanes, but what's the one up there? The one with the propeller-thingies?" Tina asked, pointing to a large model plane, dangling from the ceiling near their table. Glen rolled his eyes at Jan.

"Propeller-thingies? Where did you find this uncivilized woman? It's a C-130 turboprop. A cargo plane. Jan, didn't I take you on a C-130 when we were stationed in Virginia?"

Jan frowned. "Are you sure it wasn't when we were in Germany?"

"No. Wasn't that a Starlifter?"

Their debate was put on hold when the waiter came over to take their order. Tina asked for a Denver omelet and raised her eyebrows in surprise when Jan and her dad ordered chicken-fried steak and eggs.

"D'you two have a busy day of lumberjacking ahead of you?"

"It's the best thing on their menu," Jan said, emptying a couple of sugar packets into her coffee. "You're going to be jealous when you smell it, but don't ask for a bite. I've seen how you eat." Jan bit her lip and looked down at her coffee mug, apparently hearing the double meaning in her words only after she'd spoken them out loud. Tina covered the awkward moment by asking Glen about another airplane.

Tina continued to move the conversation along, giving prompts based on the pictures she had seen in the apartment and her growing interest in Glen's aviation knowledge. He could recite details and specs for most of the planes, but she most liked the way he added his personal stories to the dry information. Stories culled from thirty years in the air force, but most often about trips or air shows he and Jan had experienced together.

Tina glanced outside as a flash of movement caught her eye. A small blue-and-white plane took off, a speck of color against the dark clouds and the pine-covered ridge bordering the far side of the runway.

"Wish we had better weather today," Glen said, looking outside as well. "There won't be much air traffic since it's so overcast."

"This is light traffic?" Tina asked. "I've seen at least four planes take off while we've been sitting here. What?" she asked when she saw Jan and Glen smile at each other.

"It's the same plane," Jan said. "The pilot's doing touch-and-gos. Practicing takeoffs and landings."

Tina squinted out the window. "Are you sure? Wasn't the last one a different color?"

"If by a different color you mean the same blue-and-white color, then yes, it was," Glen said with a laugh. He started to explain how to identify private aircraft by shape and size while Jan excused herself. As soon as she left the table, Tina held up her hand to interrupt.

"I need to ask you something," she said, her voice serious. She wasn't sure she wanted Jan to hear this part of the conversation, so she needed to hurry and fit it in.

Glen nodded. "Go ahead."

"What would make someone who loved fighter planes and worked hard to become a pilot give up his chance and, instead, fly a…I forgot what Jan called it. A gas station with wings."

Glen raised his eyebrows in surprise. "Someone's been going through my things."

"Jan showed me some photos, and I happened to see some paperwork at the same time," Tina said quickly. She wouldn't be sidetracked. "Orders to report for flight school for the fighter jet, and a second set the following year, for the tanker. I've noticed all the pictures in your apartment. I recognize passion when I see it, and I'm curious about why you'd give up a lifelong dream."

Glen glanced toward the bathroom. "I've never told Jan about this," he said. "Our nomadic lifestyle was hard enough on her. I didn't want to add any misplaced guilt." He sighed and tapped his fingers, pausing briefly before he rushed through the story. "You see, Jan's mother was much younger than I, and back then, I was single-minded in my goal to fly fighters. The military life sounded romantic until she actually had to live it, all the moving and the long hours I had to work while I was building my career. I suggested we have a baby, foolishly thinking she'd be less lonely with a family." Glen shook his head. "A bad reason behind the best decision I ever made. Anyway, once she got pregnant, I could tell it had been a mistake for my wife. I knew my marriage was falling apart, and I just had a sense I would be left to take care of the baby on my own. My wife left before Jan's second birthday."

Tina took a sip of her coffee while Glen paused in his story. She didn't want to be tied down, to be responsible for a child, but still, she couldn't imagine walking away if she had one. Leaving a young daughter. Leaving *Jan*. Inconceivable.

"You need to understand, I didn't turn my back on my dream to fly the F-15. The dream left me. The moment I held my little girl in my arms, my old priorities simply disappeared, and she took their place. I called in some favors and was moved to the KC-135 program because it was less dangerous, and I could keep Jan with me whenever I was transferred. I still got to be around the fighters, doing my part to help them go places, but at night, I went home, where I belonged."

The waiter came and set heaping plates of food in front of them. Tina sniffed. Jan's breakfast *did* smell good. She reached across and cut a piece of steak, smearing the gravy around to conceal her theft

"You're likely to lose a hand doing that," Glen warned before he continued. "In hindsight, I should have let go of my dream of flying altogether, gotten out of the force as soon as I could and given her a stable home."

"Maybe," Tina said. She understood how Jan's childhood had affected her, with its loneliness and instability and constant change. "But she's the woman she is because of the decisions you made. And, I think you'll agree, she's pretty wonderful. And the way she teaches, finding so many ways to connect what the kids learn in the classroom to the other parts of their lives. Would she be the same kind of teacher if she hadn't been exposed to all those different places and people and ideas?"

Jan walked toward her dad and Tina, the two obviously having an intense conversation given their expressions and the way they leaned toward each other. "What are you talking…Did you steal my food?"

"Told you," Glen murmured.

"Looks the same as it did when the waiter brought it," Tina said. "Doesn't it, Glen?"

"You're on your own with this one," Glen said as Jan sat down again.

Jan glared at Tina, who seemed to be trying to assume an innocent expression. She wasn't very good at it. "You owe me some of your omelet," she said.

"Why don't we just trade. I'll give you my omelet, and I'll eat the rest of your breakfast since it got kind of messy…on the way here from the kitchen."

Jan swatted at Tina's hand when she tried to grab her plate. She reached for the ketchup bottle. "You're only being noble because I was right. I made the better breakfast choice, just like I chose the best cupcakes in Coeur d'Alene."

"Is she always this smug?" Tina asked Glen.

Jan prodded her dad in the ribs to keep him from answering. "I'll give you another bite if you just admit I was right," she said to Tina.

Tina grimaced. "After you drowned it in ketchup? No thanks."

"You have no taste," she said, taking a big bite and chewing while she looked out the window. She pointed to the north. "Look, a helicopter."

Tina checked outside before turning back to Jan with a grin. "Is this like your old *Look, a bird!* line?"

Jan laughed, glad they were able to joke about last Saturday's abbreviated trip. She had worried Tina might still be upset with her, but during their short phone conversation to set this date and so far today, she had seemed nothing but cheerful. "No, it's not. See the tall clump of trees on the ridge? Look to the right of them."

"Sure enough," Tina said. "A tiny dot in the sky."

"R-22," Glen said. "Hey, pumpkin, do you remember when we took the helicopter tour in Hawaii?"

He told Tina the whole story, with Jan chiming in occasionally, while they ate. She loved seeing her dad happy and laughing and full of memories. She wanted him to be this way forever. As she had come to expect, the intrusion of worry about the future gave her a tight feeling behind her eyes, but she blinked back the threat of tears and kept a forced smile on her face. The slight brush of a leg against hers made her look up and meet Tina's eyes. A brief press against her calf before Tina moved away again. The small gesture, the reassurance of Tina's smile, was comforting. Not something to get used to, but nice, nonetheless.

Tina asked another question and listened with what seemed to be genuine interest as her dad explained the technical aspects of airplane-wing design. Jan watched her as she seemed to mentally process the information, as if she were filing it away for later use. And it probably would show up again at some point—in her life, her work, her music. Changed, improved, embellished beyond recognition. She had exactly the quality Jan tried to instill in her students. She seemed to love to learn, regardless of the topic, and had the talent to soak up information and images. And make them her own. Jan had gotten glimpses of the way Tina's mind recreated ideas during their conversations and through the work she had been doing for Peter, and she recognized her own growing, and frightening, fascination with Tina. She could handle—and fight—a physical response to her. But being drawn to her intellectually was an entirely different, and entirely dangerous, phenomenon.

Jan picked up the bill when the waiter brought it to their table, but Tina snatched it out of her hand. "I'm paying," she announced. "It's the least I can do since you two are giving me a place to stay."

"Plus, you ate some of my breakfast," Jan said as they left the restaurant.

"One bite," Tina protested. "And you never did prove it was me and not the waiter. Hey, an old menu."

Jan peered over her shoulder at the bulletin board full of ads for planes, flying lessons, and airplane parts. In the middle was a framed copy of the restaurant's original menu. Jan read the faded print. "Meatloaf, twenty-five cents. A piece of pie for a nickel."

"What a great look for Peter's website and ads," Tina said. She frowned and her gaze was distant as she thought out loud. "Something about eating like it was yesterday, or at yesterday's prices."

"You can have prices listed like a menu," Jan said. "Carrot seeds or tomato plants on one side, with a comparison of what you'd have to pay for the fruits or vegetables in a grocery store on the other."

"I like it," Tina said. "I'm picturing a faded, yellowish background, like old paper."

"It fits with your old-fashioned general store theme."

"Yes, and Peter will love it. How's this," Tina turned to face her, the excitement of inspiration evident on her face. "Tomorrow's dinner at yesterday's prices."

"Perfect," Jan said. She fell silent, awed by the intensity of Tina's focus when she was creating like this. Her dad cleared his throat, and she took a step back like a guilty teenager caught out after curfew. Tina moved back as well.

"You two make a good team," Glen said, an innocent expression on his face.

Jan frowned at him as she brushed by on her way to the door. "Let's go," she said, concerned because she had been thinking the same thing.

❖

Jan picked up her phone for what felt like the hundredth time, and then she put it down again. Tuesday afternoon. Her classes were wearing her out as she dealt with frantic students trying to cram a semester's worth of questions into less than a month of class, edgy seniors who knew they were only days away from freedom, and masses of projects and assignments to grade. No matter how prepared she was, the last few weeks of school were always stressful and unpredictable. A night out would be good for her. A night out with Tina would be even better. She felt the echo of the camaraderie they'd shared at the airport. The connection had felt good. Not just between her and Tina, but between Tina and her dad, too.

Her dad liked Tina. Maybe too much, because he was turning into as determined a matchmaker as Brooke. He had been mentioning Tina at every opportunity, suggesting Jan call her and have an evening out. Jan had argued at first, but now she was changing her mind. Missing Tina's company. She could watch Tina play at O'Boyle's.

Challenge her to a rematch at pool. Maybe flirt a little. Maybe flirt a lot…What could it hurt?

Unfortunately, Jan knew exactly how much it could hurt. So she kept putting her phone away. But she also knew how she felt around Tina, and how much she longed to touch her. If she went into the night with no expectations beyond an evening of play and sex and fun, maybe she could come out the other side unscarred. Maybe…

She picked up her phone and punched in Tina's number. A few rings later, Tina answered, the sounds of talking and laughter in the background.

"Hey you," Tina said. Jan's cynical side wondered who was with Tina, keeping her from saying Jan's name on the phone.

"Hey yourself. I'm going to the pub tonight with Chloe. Any chance I'll see you there?"

"No, sorry. I'm actually in Seattle. I thought of a cool idea for a website, and I came over here to pitch it to a couple of businesses. And to spend a few days in the big city."

Jan forced herself to echo Tina's laughter. *Why didn't you let me know you were leaving Spokane?* she wanted to ask. But what reason did Tina have to explain her actions to Jan? "Sounds like fun," she said out loud. "Well, have a safe trip back."

"Will do. Talk to you later."

Jan disconnected and leaned her elbows on her desk. She felt hurt that Tina hadn't shared any of this with her. She hadn't told Jan about her website idea, but why should she? Just because they had brainstormed together once and seemed in sync with their ideas, she had no reason to expect Tina to discuss any other work-related issues with her. And just because Tina was staying at her dad's apartment, she had no reason to tell Jan when she'd be sleeping elsewhere. Jan dropped her forehead against her hands. No, the big problem wasn't that Tina hadn't told her these things. It was that Jan wanted to know. She had started to care about Tina—her life, her job, her thoughts—and that kind of caring would only get her hurt. Sexual attraction might be reciprocated, but not *caring*. She needed to remember that, if she was going to get through the rest of Tina's stay in Spokane without losing her heart completely.

CHAPTER TEN

Tina stared at the phone in her hand. "You okay?" Brooke asked as she came into the kitchen.

"Yeah, fine. Some mockups for my cousin's newspaper ads are ready," Tina lied. She stole a stuffed mushroom off the tray Brooke pulled out of the fridge and followed her into the living room, where Andy and the other members of their quartet sprawled on various pieces of furniture. She had lied to both Brooke and Jan. Brooke, because she had been after Tina all day with questions about Jan, and Tina hadn't figured out how to distract her from her matchmaking obsession. And Jan, because she couldn't let her know how shaken she'd been after a simple breakfast with her and Glen. Watching their affectionate and playful interaction, bouncing ideas off someone intelligent and quick and understanding, feeling a little like part of a family. But a family unlike her own, with its complex web of responsibility and guilt and regret. That morning had scared the crap out of her, and she had run away like a chicken. And, damn it, all she wanted to do now was speed back to Spokane just for a chance to watch Jan play pool at O'Boyle's.

She hadn't been lying about her business meetings, however. Glen's talk about planes had triggered Tina's memory of her drive to Spokane. The angled blades of windmills, the arched wings of ducks sailing over her car to land in a lake on the side of the freeway, the curve of an airplane wing's leading edge. She had gone directly back to the apartment and used some of Jan's lesson-planning techniques to develop the outline for an entire PR package. A little research online had given her the names of several aviation-related businesses with poorly designed and hard-to-navigate sites. A few queries later, and she had lined up interviews with two aeronautical engineering firms. She'd use the hefty advance she'd received from the one she had finally signed to take Jan and her dad out for a nice dinner, as a thank you. Or, maybe, send them out to dinner without her. The safer option.

"Come sit by me," David, the group's cellist, said, with an exaggerated wink in Brooke's direction when Tina came into the living room. He scooted over to make space between him and his partner Jonas. "I want to hear every detail about the evening you spent in a pub with Jan. You know we're all rooting for you two crazy kids to get together."

So Brooke was enlisting accomplices in her matchmaking battle. Tina could only think of one way to end the war. "The bar's called O'Boyle's," she said as she sat on the couch next to David. "Jan came with her friend Chloe…"

❖

Tina tapped her fingers impatiently on the table at O'Boyle's, out of rhythm with the jazz combo playing on the small stage. She hoped the directions she had given Andy and Brooke were sufficiently convoluted, but her knowledge of Spokane was too limited for her to be sure. She was fairly certain she had them circling the airport on the way to the pub, and she'd have to count on traffic to buy her some time. Only a week after her visit to Seattle, they had called from just outside Spokane, on their way to a hotel. A last-minute wedding cancellation had given Andy a rare weekend off, and the two of them had decided to spring a surprise visit on Tina and Jan. Surprise inspection was more like it. Tina stood up and waved the moment she saw Jan step through the door.

"Is everything okay?" Jan asked as she shrugged out of her coat and sat across from Tina. "Your message sounded very dramatic, but when you wanted to meet in a bar…"

"Drink this, and then I'll explain," Tina said, sliding a shot glass filled with amber liquid in front of Jan.

"What is it?" Jan sniffed the glass and took a small sip.

"Oh my God. It's a shot of whiskey, not tea with the queen. Just drink it."

"You're acting crazy," Jan said, but she drank the whiskey in several gulps, stopping to cough after each one.

"Really? And you claim you went to college?" Tina asked with a laugh. "I'll have to teach you how drink a shot someday, but we don't have time now. Brooke and Andy are on their way here to surprise you."

"Oh, how nice," Jan said, setting the glass on the table. "I haven't seen them since last Christmas when—"

"They think we're dating," Tina said. Might as well get right to the point. Jan looked at her with an expression of shock and disbelief. Should have gotten her two drinks, not just one. Tina pushed her own shot of whiskey toward her.

"Why would they think that?" Jan asked, gulping down half. Her shot-drinking ability was improving.

"I might have told them…Stop looking at me like that and let me explain. I saw them when I was in Seattle, and Brooke wouldn't stop asking about us. So I had a great idea…" It had seemed like one when she was in a different city. Faking a relationship with Jan when they were a few hundred miles apart was easy. Sitting next to her and discussing a relationship? Distracting, to say the least. She should feel claustrophobic. Instead, she felt…*tempted.* And scared as hell. "Instead of fighting her on this, I let her think we're going out."

"You *lied*? You know how Brooke is. She'll never let this go—"

"Would you talk less and drink more so I can explain? The way I see it, if we keep refusing to be set up, she'll just keep pushing harder. But if we date for a few weeks, and it doesn't work out, she'll know we tried and will finally let us be. Brilliant plan, isn't it? I'm a genius."

Jan didn't look convinced. She took another sip of Tina's drink. "So how long do we have to keep this up?"

"I wasn't expecting them to come over this weekend. I figured we would have had our fake breakup before we saw them in person again. You know Brooke. For all her meddling, she does want to make people feel comfortable. She'll go out of her way to keep us apart if she thinks we're heartbroken over a failed relationship."

"Have you *ever* been heartbroken at the end of a relationship? How sad can you be after knowing someone two days?"

"Very funny. Fine, we'll wait at least a couple weeks before you break up with me. That'll teach me a lesson, after all these years of playing the field," Tina said. She pulled her glass out of Jan's hands and finished it off. She had been a mass of confused thoughts since Andy had called her a few hours earlier. The idea of pretending to be Jan's girlfriend for a few hours had seemed uncomfortably appealing. Planning their breakup was more disconcerting than she liked. Telling Jan about the idea? Terrifying. "I should have ordered more of these."

Jan flagged down a waitress and ordered more whiskey. "So, what's our story?" she asked after the waitress left, their two empty glasses on her tray.

"The details are the same. Drinks in the Peacock Room, here, Coeur d'Alene..." Tina said, trying to remember the details she had given Brooke. "But we kissed."

"When we were playing pool," Jan said.

"When we were on the pier," Tina said at the same time. She pictured Jan leaning over to take a shot. "Yours is better. I should have gone with that."

"So..." Jan prompted.

"So? That's all I said. We made out on the boardwalk, and we're sort of dating. But it's all so new, we'd been hesitant to share our news until Brooke and the others dragged it out of me in Seattle. Eventually we'll fight and break up. Then we're free," Tina said. Where were those drinks?

"We made out in public? Romantic," Jan said with a snort. "No wonder we're breaking up."

"Okay, I gave you a chaste peck on the cheek, then ran to a florist in Coeur d'Alene and bought you a dozen red roses and a heart-shaped box of candy. Last night we sat on the porch swing and held hands. Better?"

"You should have said it started here in the bar. I would've made out with you then. Hypothetically."

Tina's mouth was suddenly dry. Jan's voice was casual, but her expression was anything but. Over and over, Tina had imagined their game of pool ending differently. It never occurred to her Jan might have done the same thing. She pictured Jan in bed, naked between the sheets, moonlight filtering in through her curtains…thinking of Tina. Touching the places Tina wanted to touch. Eliciting the responses Tina wanted to hear and smell and taste. Tina blinked, pushing aside the image of fantasy-Jan trembling under her touch and trying to focus on what the real Jan was saying to her.

"So tonight we're expected to act like we're…" Jan hesitated. "Dating?"

"Lovers," Tina said.

"At what point does Mr. Roper come in?" Jan asked. She paused while the waitress delivered their drinks. "Something bad is going to happen. I'm not good at ad-libbing like this."

"Well, we don't have time to rehearse," Tina said. She had been watching the door and saw the moment Brooke and Andy came in. "Here they are. Sweetie."

"Did you call me *sweetie*?" Jan asked as she took both drinks from the waitress. "Can I change that, or did you already tell Brooke?"

❖

"I've been warned you're a pool shark," Andy said as she chalked her cue.

Jan racked the balls and wished she had drunk more of Tina's whiskey. After the first awkward moments when Andy and Brooke arrived, she had relaxed and started to enjoy what felt like a simple evening with friends, laughing and catching up on the news from Seattle. She had almost forgotten Tina's ridiculous ruse until Andy had suggested a pool game. As if she and Brooke were trying to separate the happy couple and grill them individually. "I've been called a hustler, but we don't need to bet any money on the game."

Andy looked at her with that intense grin Jan had seen before. "Are you calling me chicken?" she asked, slapping a twenty on the table.

"Hey, if you want to lose your money," Jan said, waving off the rest of the sentence. "Why don't you break."

The balls broke evenly, but nothing dropped. "So, you and Tina are dating," Andy said, leaning against the corner of the table while Jan lined up her shot.

"Yeah," Jan said. She smacked the cue ball with too much force. She sank the fourteen but had no second shot. "Stripes," she said as she tapped the nine and buried the cue ball.

"Clever," Andy said, walking around the table and looking at her options. "And when did this start?"

Something in Andy's tone made Jan wary. She had to admit she wasn't the most spontaneous of people. Sitting at the table with Tina's arm across the back of her chair had been easy enough. Comfortable, while the three of them talked, even though she was overly conscious of Tina's closeness. But, now, when she was expected to make up details under Andy's all-too-perceptive gaze? Jan was about to break and tell all their secrets. Only Tina's occasional glare, from where she sat at the table with Brooke, kept Jan from cracking completely.

"It was during a day trip we took to Lake Coeur d'Alene. We were on the boardwalk, and she kissed me. It was so romantic," Jan said, realizing it sounded dull, and not very romantic, when she spoke in such a monotone. The actual walk they took, etched into her memory, had been anything but boring, anything but chaste. Holding Tina in her arms had affected her more than she cared to admit. The bland lie was easier to deal with than the truth.

"Sounds like poetry," Andy observed, her eyes on the pool table.

"My heart skipped a beat, and I heard a choir of angels," Jan said as Andy sank the three on a lucky shot. "Are we allowing slop?" she asked. "You didn't call the shot, and I know you were aiming at the five."

"Seems to me, we're letting a lot of things slide tonight," Andy said. She dropped the six ball in the corner pocket. "You know I love Tina, but I have to admit she's a player. How'd you manage to capture her heart?"

Jan dropped the twelve in a side pocket with a decisive smack after Andy missed a shot on the four. She peered down her cue stick at the thirteen. "Just lucky, I guess. How're you managing without her in your quartet?"

"Oh, we're doing quite well. Our temporary second violinist will be a fine replacement if Tina decides to stay in Spokane. Since she's so in *looooove*." Andy drew the last word out for several syllables before she started laughing.

Jan missed her shot by a wide margin and stood up, frowning at Andy. "What, you don't think I'm attractive enough for someone like Tina?"

Andy shrugged. "I think you're stunning. And exactly the kind of woman Tina needs," she said as she sank the one but only grazed the two, leaving Jan without a shot. "I just find it hard to believe *she* realizes it."

"Well, she does," Jan said as she sank the ten in an impossibly tricky bank shot. She struggled to find a way to express her pretend relationship with Tina to this woman who was so obviously in love with Brooke. Andy would see right through any lies she told, so she stuck with the uncomfortable truth. "She makes me feel sexy, and it's all I can do to keep my hands off her whenever we're together," she said, sinking the nine on her second try at it. The fifteen followed right after. "And she challenges me to be more than I am. To be spontaneous and relaxed and living in the moment." The thirteen dropped into a corner pocket, nearly followed by the cue ball since Jan hit it so hard. Luckily, it caught the edge of the pocket and caromed back toward the center of the table. "And I can't stop thinking about her, even when I'm supposed to be in class or at the store or talking to someone else." Jan knocked in the eleven.

"Well, you've convinced me," Andy said with a low whistle. "It just seemed pretty convenient that you and Tina suddenly started dating the minute she came to Spokane. After spending two years refusing to be in the same room."

"What can I say? We finally had a chance to get to know each other." Jan wondered if she was laying it on too thick, especially since they'd need to break up soon. And believably. "But we are such different people, and like you said, Tina's a player. Who knows how long this will last?"

Andy shrugged. "Who knows?" she echoed.

Jan tapped her cue stick near a side pocket. "Eight ball right here, and you stop hounding me about Tina. You can even keep your twenty." She hit the cue ball against the edge of the table and it angled back to the black eight, tapping it gently into the designated pocket.

"Nice," said Andy. "All right. You and Tina are a cute couple, and I don't have any doubts about your relationship. Plus, you can have the money. You earned it."

Tina and Brooke walked over to the pool table as Jan was pocketing her money. Tina draped an arm around Jan's shoulders. She had been spending the evening trying to look like Jan's girlfriend without being more physical than she thought either one of them could handle. No hands roaming beyond arms or shoulders, and definitely no kissing. She remembered the boardwalk and the feeling of Jan's arms around her. She stood close for Brooke's benefit but held herself stiffly, so her body barely made contact with Jan's "Did you win, sweetie?" Jan glared at her and she tried again. "Honey? Sweetheart?"

Jan finally laughed and playfully pushed Tina away. "My students call me Ms. Carroll. That'll do."

"Okay, teacher," Tina said in her most seductive voice as she scooted closer to Jan. She didn't mind a chance to play along with one of her fantasies. "How can I earn some extra credit?"

"Do we really have to listen to this crap?" Andy asked.

"Oh, I think it's cute," Brooke said, her arms looped around Andy's neck. "It's nice to see them so in love."

Tina looked at her suspiciously. She had seemed to drag the word out longer than necessary. Jan tugged on her arm, distracting her.

"Why don't you and Andy play this round," Jan said to Brooke. "Babycakes and I will go get drinks."

"Babycakes?" Tina asked once they were standing at the bar. "Are you serious?"

"Shut up," Jan said. "They know we're not dating. At least Andy does. And if she knows something, Brooke does, too."

Tina tapped her fingers on the counter as she watched her two friends playing pool. They seemed more interested in playing with each other than actually making effective shots. "I thought Brooke seemed kind of funny when we were talking. I expected her to be happier because she had finally brought us together, but she barely talked about it. But they don't—"

Jan took her by the shoulders and gave her a little shake. "If you say they don't know we know they know, I am walking right out that door," she said in a threatening voice. "What are we supposed to do now?"

Tina shrugged, pushing against Jan's hands and feeling a strange sense of comfort in their weight. Jan increased the pressure for a brief moment, a gentle squeeze, before letting go and breaking the connection. "We go back to the pool table and take them for all the cash they have on hand," she said, giving Jan a swat on the rear. "That is, if you can concentrate on pool with me around."

Jan picked up two of the drinks the bartender put in front of them. "I think I proved how little you distract me during our last pool game," she said.

"During the game, yes," Tina said, moving into Jan's space. And not just because Brooke and Andy were looking their way. She ran her fingers through Jan's silky hair and watched it drift back against her cheek, her neck. "But what about later that night when you were alone? Was I a distraction then?"

Jan's blush confirmed Tina's suspicion. Jan had been as turned on that night as she had. Jan opened her mouth as if to answer, but she closed it again without saying a word and walked away, leaving Tina to take care of the other drinks. And the tab.

CHAPTER ELEVEN

"You're early," Jan said when she cracked the door the next morning and peered around it at Tina. She had been planning to meet everyone for lunch, and having Tina show up on her doorstep—before she had even gotten dressed—wasn't her idea of a great start to the day.

"Well, good morning to you, too, snuggle bunny," Tina said, taking a paper cup of coffee out of the carrier she was holding and passing it through the narrow opening.

"Ugh, those pet names of yours are getting worse," Jan said. She took an appreciative sniff of the vanilla-scented coffee, but she wasn't about to be bought with caffeine. She kept the door open just enough to show her face. "Thanks for the coffee, and I'll see you later."

She was about to shut the door when her dad walked up behind her. "Who are you…Oh, hello, Tina."

"Hi, Glen," Tina said. "I brought you a cup of coffee, but your daughter won't let me in."

"That's because she's still in her pajamas," he said.

"Dad!"

She turned her attention away from the door for just a moment, and Tina took advantage of the opportunity to push her way inside. "You won't hear any complaints from me," she said as she handed Glen his coffee and the newspaper from the front porch.

"I didn't think I would," he said as he accepted Tina's offerings. "Thank you, my dear. I'll be in the kitchen."

Jan crossed her arms tightly over her chest. Her boxer shorts and tank top felt insignificant under Tina's gaze. The flimsy material seemed to disintegrate when Tina merely looked at her, leaving her naked. Too exposed. "Okay, you delivered your coffees. Now go, and I'll see you at lunch. Or are you waiting for a tip?"

"I wouldn't mind one, but we don't have time for that right now. There's been a change in plans."

Jan groaned. Plans were made for a reason. So everyone would know what to expect from the day. "What kind of change?"

"There's a bluegrass festival in Wenatchee. We decided the four of us should go, and Brooke and Andy will just drive home from there. Small-town thing, tons of music and food. It'll be a blast."

"Wenatchee?" Jan asked, certain she hadn't heard correctly. "A six-hour round-trip just to hear some people play the banjo?"

"Just to…Wow, are you in for a treat. And a musical education. Now get dressed because Brooke and Andy already have an hour head start."

"We were going to have lunch near Gonzaga and walk around the campus," Jan said, trying to sound as reasonable as possible since Tina was obviously going insane. Why'd she have to be so damned adorable when she acted so crazy? "I don't have time for more than that. I have to grade class projects, prepare the final exam…and what if Dad needs me?"

"Then he'll call, and we'll come straight home. And you can do the rest tomorrow. Besides, you're the one who's always ten lesson plans ahead, I'm sure you already have the final finished up here."

Jan swatted at Tina's hand when she tapped her on the forehead, and then she recrossed her arms. "Maybe we can just move our schedule up a few weeks and tell them we broke up. They can console you at the festival while I stay at home and get my work done."

"You know, when you cross your arms, you're not really hiding anything. You're just pushing your breasts together. Now go get dressed. I'm not leaving without you."

Jan eased the tension in her arms and turned away to hide her embarrassment. She had a feeling Tina was as stubborn as she sounded. Jan could either argue more or just save them both some time and go along with the new plan. Either way, she wanted to be fully clothed. "I'll get dressed," she conceded. She started up the stairs with Tina on her heels. "You wait here."

"Yes, ma'am," Tina said. She watched Jan jog up the steps before she turned away. Before she *could* turn away. Those satiny boxer shorts, sitting low on Jan's slender hips, and the tiny tank top had left just enough to the imagination. Tina considered trotting up the stairs after her, but she decided to obey Jan's order to wait below. She went into the kitchen and found Glen at the table, struggling to open his paper with one good arm.

Tina took the sports page from him and carefully folded it into an easy-to-manage rectangle. "Thank you," he said, propping it on a small vase. "I'm getting mighty tired of doing everything with one hand."

"I'll bet," she said, pulling out a chair and sitting down. She cradled her hands around her mocha and watched him for a few moments. He looked normal and sounded normal, but she didn't know him well enough to recognize any small signs of change. "I've come to kidnap your daughter for the day."

"Have at it," Glen said. "It'll be good for her to get out and have some fun for a change."

"Will you be okay?"

"Well, I won't be as neat with the paper as you were, but I'll get by," he said with a smile. Tina kept silent until he sighed and pulled a small laminated card from the front of his shirt. It was looped around his neck on a cord. "My name and address, and Jan's information. I wear it everywhere now, even to bed." He shrugged. "I don't think I need it yet, but I know it gives her some peace of mind. Besides, I'm going golfing with some old air force buddies today."

"Golfing?" Tina asked skeptically.

"Don't worry," he said with a wry smile. "I do remember you need two good arms to play. But the walking will do me good. And I'll be free to give the guys pointers while they play."

"I'm sure they'll appreciate the help," Tina said with a laugh. "Just remember to duck if one of them comes at you with his club."

She slid a piece of paper across the table. "This is my cell number, and my cousin Peter's, too," she said. She had been surprised by how easy it was to ask a favor from family when it wasn't personal but was meant to help Jan. And gratified by how quick Peter was to assure her he'd be there for Glen if necessary. "He'll be at the nursery all day, just a few minutes from here, in case you need anything."

Glen thanked her and tucked the paper in his shirt pocket just as Jan came into the kitchen. Tan cotton shorts and a pale pink T-shirt had replaced the skimpier ensemble. Just as sexy. Damn. Tina had to give up the illusion that she had only been turned on because of Jan's boxer shorts and tank, not the woman inside. But Jan could have duct taped brown paper bags on her body, and she'd have looked just as sexy.

"Do you have a change of clothes in case you get cold?" Tina asked. She had a jacket and jeans in the trunk of her car since she was expecting a cooler evening in the foothills of the Cascades.

"In here," Jan said, shrugging her shoulder, a stuffed backpack hanging off it.

"What do you want to bet she has schoolwork in there, too?" Tina asked Glen.

"I'll keep my money, thanks. You have a good time, pumpkin."

Jan fussed over her dad, soliciting his promise to send a text when he got home from golf and explaining exactly how long he should microwave last night's chicken dinner, until Tina finally managed to herd her out the door and into the car. Jan sat in the passenger seat and fidgeted. She had agreed to come because who knew when she'd have a chance to see Brooke again? And since she and Andy had already left for the festival, she couldn't make them drive back to Spokane. She tried to put the extra work she'd need to do tomorrow out of her mind and focus on going with the flow for once.

Tina pushed firmly on her knee. "Stop bouncing. Your dad will be fine, and you're going to have fun. Besides, it's our very first road trip together," she added in her best Chloe-in-love voice.

Jan laughed and felt herself relax a little bit. "Our second. You're forgetting Coeur d'Alene."

"I'm not forgetting it at all. We just weren't fake-dating then."

"Of course. You can probably let go of my leg now," she said since Tina hadn't moved her hand off Jan's knee. "I doubt Brooke is doing surveillance of your car to make sure we're acting like a couple."

"I'm practicing method acting," Tina said, but she shifted her hand to the steering wheel. "Trying to get deep into my character's motivation."

"I'm afraid to ask what that might be," Jan said. Tina just waggled her eyebrows suggestively, and Jan punched her lightly on the arm. "Attention on the road," she ordered.

She wouldn't have minded continuing their playful game, since she knew the feelings between them were safely in the realm of make-believe, but Tina turned to more serious topics as she accelerated onto the freeway.

"Your dad seems in good spirits," she said, her eyes on the road. "Is he really this cheerful, or is he trying to pretend everything's okay so you don't worry?"

Jan shrugged. "A little of both, I guess. You've seen him at his best because he likes you, and he's always been very pragmatic. But he's had a couple of memory slips that led to fights because he got frustrated and I got frightened. I suppose I don't hide my feelings well enough—"

"Do *not* blame yourself for any of this," Tina said firmly, reaching over and grabbing Jan's hand. "You're doing the best you can. You both are."

Jan squeezed Tina's fingers in thanks. Tina kept hold of her hand while Jan went on to talk about what the doctors had told her and her dad to expect in the future, and what decisions they'd need to make together. Tina prompted her occasionally with gentle questions, and Jan slowly let herself open up more about her fears and concerns. She had been keeping most of them inside, and the simple act of sharing was a huge relief. And Tina's logic and compassion as they debated some of the choices facing Jan was a comfort. Tina was a temporary, pretend girlfriend, unwilling to be held down by any woman—let alone one facing an uncertain future—but Jan decided to accept the simplicity of what she was offering. Jan had a full day to be someone else, someone with a partner to share her burdens and with no agenda, except to have fun. She'd take advantage of every moment of it. She slipped her fingers between Tina's, locking their hands together.

"What about you?" she asked. "How's your family life?"

Tina shrugged. She was prepared for the usual tightening in her stomach she felt whenever the topic came up, but she didn't feel it this time. Probably because too much of her attention was focused on the soft thigh under her hand. She checked over her shoulder for traffic before changing lanes so she had an excuse to move her hand a little farther up Jan's lap. "I've seen my grandmother a couple times at the nursery, and the police haven't been called, so I guess you could say we're doing as well as can be expected."

Tina thought back to those two brief meetings. After her initial arrival in Spokane, she had been upset and looking for a fight. When Francine had stopped by a week later and commented on one of Tina's designs, Tina had gone on the defensive, hearing criticism in every word. Only Peter's pleadings, when he caught up to her in the parking lot, had kept her from just getting in her car and heading straight to Seattle. The second time, Tina had nearly bumped into her grandmother as they came around a display of flowering shrubs. A civil exchange of greetings had been the entirety of their conversation. It was the most pleasant one Tina could remember ever having with her.

"I've liked seeing my aunt and uncle again," she continued, rubbing her thumb lightly over the back of Jan's hand. "And Peter has become…a friend."

Jan laughed and squeezed her hand. "And you sound upset about it."

"More like surprised," Tina admitted. She and her cousin were enough alike to make them compatible, but their friendship had grown beyond what she'd anticipated from a relative. Their business meetings often turned into personal conversations, and she had come to appreciate his intelligence, his dry sense of humor, and their shared passion for music. "I'll actually miss him when I leave."

She thought she felt Jan stiffen at her words, but her voice was calm when she asked Tina about the work she was doing for the aeronautics company. Tina wanted to say she'd miss Jan, too, when she left Spokane, but somehow the words didn't express how she really felt. Instead, she stayed on the safe topics of her design business and Jan's school until they reached the small town of Wenatchee.

❖

"I can take a hint," Brooke said, interrupting Jan's focus on the two women in front of her. Tina and Andy had stopped to watch one of the many impromptu jam sessions they had seen at the festival. It seemed everyone had an instrument and was willing to play it at the slightest sign of encouragement. The blend of different styles of bluegrass—from country to urban—and the chaos, as scheduled performances competed with spur-of-the-moment tunes, ought to have been a cacophonous assault on her ears, but instead, Jan felt comfortably enveloped by the music of the festival.

"Okay," Jan said, her attention on Tina's expressive fingers as she argued with Andy. They were clearly discussing some matter of technique as they gestured and played air violins. Jan could almost feel Tina's desire to have a real fiddle in her hands. "Wait, what?"

"I'll stop meddling. You and Tina proved your point."

"Good," Jan said. "What point?"

"You don't want me involved in your social lives."

"Well, we don't." Jan still felt she had missed part of Brooke's conversation. Her comments seemed to have come from out of the blue. "How exactly did we prove it to you?"

"The whole pretending-to-be-dating thing. I get it, and I won't try to set the two of you up again."

Jan considered protesting more vigorously, since she knew Tina would want her to, but she couldn't see the point. She and Tina simply weren't believable as a couple. She had always known they weren't. "What a relief," Jan eventually said, giving up the charade in a not very relieved sounding voice. She wondered briefly if they needed to tell Tina yet. Jan had actually been enjoying the afternoon. Tina's occasional touch on her shoulder or back, her attentiveness, her closeness. "What gave us away? Those stupid pet names she kept making up?"

"No," Brooke said with a wave of her hand. "Those were adorable. They made you smile every time, so she kept coming up with sillier ones. But something just didn't seem right. I guess love just can't be faked."

"I thought we were pretty convincing," Jan muttered as she started walking faster. Brooke matched her long stride.

"Are you angry? I'm not insulting your acting skills, I'm just saying I understand. And the good thing is, since you and Tina are friends now, we can all hang out together when you come to Seattle."

Hang out with Tina and her date of the week. Two loving couples and Jan. "Hooray," she said as they caught up to Tina and Andy, who had stopped at a snack bar.

"Are you hungry, sex kitten?" Tina asked. "Hey, what's wrong?"

Jan frowned. She kind of liked the new name. "You can stop acting like my girlfriend. They're on to us."

"Really?" Tina asked, looking from Brooke to Andy. "I know you were suspicious last night, but I thought we were acting like a real couple today."

"Yeah, you really had us going for a while," Andy said, rolling her eyes. "Not."

Jan ignored Andy's dry remark and turned to Tina. "I thought so, too. Especially when you noticed I was cold and went to get my coat." Tina had let her hands linger in Jan's hair after she pulled it free of the coat's collar. Brushing against her neck like a warm breeze. Jan hadn't felt cold anymore, but her sudden rush of heat had nothing to do with the coat.

"And when you bought me the hand-carved fiddle stand because you knew I didn't have a place to set my violin when I practice in the apartment. It was very considerate. Something a girlfriend would do." Jan smiled at her, glad Tina had liked the little gift. When Tina had played the Cajun music for her, she had noticed she had to set the violin in its case every time she needed her hands free. The stand seemed like a convenient accessory, and the rustic carving of the piece suited Tina's style.

"Fine, you convinced me," Brooke said, raising her hands in surrender. "I believe you're really in love. When's the wedding?"

"Oh, don't patronize us," Jan said, angry because she wasn't quite sure what she was arguing for anymore.

"How about we save this discussion for later and focus on what's really important," Andy said as she moved up to the snack bar's counter. "Now, who wants french fries?"

❖

"Did you know the whole time?" Tina asked Andy once they were seated near the performance stage. Jan and Brooke had gone to get another round of snacks.

"When you told us in Seattle, I suspected you were just trying to get everyone off your back. And once I saw you with Jan, I knew for sure," Andy said. "You were very careful about how you touched each other, and you never held hands. Neither of you is a very good liar."

Tina frowned. She wasn't so sure of that. She had done a good job of convincing herself, but she wasn't about to admit it to Andy. Nor did she want to mention that they had held hands in the car, when they were alone. She had only been reserved when touching Jan in public because she didn't think she'd be able to stop once she started to let her hands roam. "But we've had fun together, like two couples."

Andy shrugged. "Like four friends."

"More fun than we ever had when I brought dates out with us," Tina continued, ignoring Andy's comment.

"Because Brooke and I know Jan. Most of the girls you've brought along were nice enough, but they were strangers to us. Hell, they were practically strangers to *you*."

"I do like her, you know," Tina said quietly. She wasn't sure how much, or what it meant, but it was too real to be ignored.

"Hey." Andy bumped her shoulder against Tina's. "That's obvious. But do you like her as in you want to spend a night with her, or do you like her as in you want to move to Spokane and help her with her dad, and stick around for all the mornings after?"

Tina was silent. Of course she meant the former. Only a fool would sign up for the lifetime option. She saw Jan and Brooke approaching and watched as Jan handed the food she was carrying to Brooke and knelt to pet an Australian Cattle Dog with a bandana around its neck. She had visited every dog at the festival—and there were almost as many of them as people—and Tina, in her girlfriend persona, had imagined a rather pleasant scene in which she gave Jan a puppy as a present. And then what? She would go back to Seattle, leaving Jan to care for her dad and a new pet all alone. Andy was right. If Tina wasn't prepared to stay long-term, she had no right to play with Jan's affection. She had to stop pretending because she had no intention of making their relationship permanent.

"Thanks," she said when Jan handed her one of the messy, greasy chili dogs she had in her hands. She was relieved when Jan chose a seat on the aisle, so the two of them were flanking Andy and Brooke and not sitting next to each other. She took a big bite and tried to swallow it even though her throat felt strangely tight.

❖

The effort to maintain small talk for the three-hour drive back to Spokane was almost painful. Jan came up with an admirable number of questions about fiddle music, styles, and history until even Tina was bored, hearing herself lecture about one of her favorite subjects. Tina did her part, as well, and she had learned more than she ever wanted to know about geometry before she finally parked in front of Jan's house. The porch light and a lamp in the living room were on, but the rest of the house was dark.

"Well, that was…a long day," Tina said awkwardly as she turned off the car and faced Jan. Even though the relationship had been a sham, its end had managed to put a stop to their playful, teasing friendship. Tina didn't know how to get it back, or even if she wanted to. Maybe it was for the best if they simply let their association fade. After all, she'd be leaving soon.

"Can you stay?"

Jan's words caught Tina by surprise. A jumble of images raced through her mind—Jan underneath her, over her, putting on her satiny boxers just so Tina could rip them off again. She pushed the thoughts aside and tried to concentrate on being the sensible one. Jan seemed better suited for the job, but she was apparently giving up her role as most practical person in the car. "I shouldn't. I mean, of course I want to, but it wouldn't be right to—"

"To lead me on?" Jan finished her sentence with a smile.

"Well, yeah."

"I'm not a fool, Tina. I know it would just be tonight. But maybe I don't want it to mean anything more, either. Maybe reality has worn me down, and I need a night of fantasy. Just one night."

Tina grabbed Jan's hand and briefly kissed her palm, her wrist. She was tempted by Jan's offer. Not because she wanted a no-strings, one-night stand. But because she was afraid to look too closely at what she *did* want. And she was just as scared at the prospect of letting Jan go. "Don't think it wouldn't mean anything. I care about you, but I..."

Jan moved her hand out of Tina's grasp, sliding it along her cheekbone and letting it rest alongside Tina's neck. She kept her touch casual, fighting the urge to trace Tina's collarbone with her fingers until she reached the buttons on her shirt. They looked easy enough to rip open. "Of course it would mean something, to both of us. But it doesn't have to mean *everything*."

Jan waited while Tina seemed to struggle with herself. Jan was patient because she had spent most of the day facing the same internal struggle, and she had finally reached her decision. Just because there was no one left to convince they were a couple didn't mean the game had to stop. Why not have a night together, too? Jan knew it was a stupid decision, knew she would be left alone and hurt after Tina went home, but she would deal with the pain later. And she would survive it. Not having this night together was a much worse option. She had gotten a small taste of being Tina's girlfriend, and she wanted more, wanted to know what it would be like to be satisfied completely with Tina. And then she'd let her go.

Tina finally leaned over and gave her a soft kiss on the cheek, lingering to rest her forehead against Jan's. "Yes, sugar dumpling. I'll spend the night."

Jan groaned and shoved her away. "First, we're going to set some ground rules about what you're allowed to call me, or I promise, I'll kick you out of bed."

CHAPTER TWELVE

Tina followed Jan up the stairs, being careful to walk softly so she wouldn't wake Jan's dad. She had imagined this scenario this morning when she had watched Jan go upstairs to get dressed. Chasing Jan up to her room, throwing her on the bed, pulling those boxers off fast and rough enough to tear them. Passionate. Exciting. She supposed she should be turned on by the memories of sneaking past a girlfriend's sleeping parents—something she hadn't done for years—but the quiet house only seemed to shout responsibility.

But, still, she didn't want to leave. She closed the door to the little bedroom behind them and leaned against it while Jan crossed the room and took off her shoes and jacket. Tina expected to be thrown into a panic in the midst of quiet preparations for bed, grown-up obligations, and the uncertainty of her future with Jan. Instead, she felt as if she was waiting, listening, like she did when she heard a new tune. Before she played it and made it her own.

Tina stayed where she was as Jan sat on the bed and watched her in silence. Jan knew her reputation, and she was probably waiting for Tina to make the first move. Usually she would. She'd initiate sex as soon as she and her girlfriend-of-the-week were behind closed doors, if not before. She always liked the women she dated, enjoyed their company at dinner and in bed, but she rarely wanted to know more about them than what kind of wine they drank or the color of their underwear. And she certainly wasn't interested in anything that meant too much or probed too deep, like how they decorated their bedrooms, how they lived and ordered their lives. She was just passing through on her way to somewhere else, and it was best to keep things shallow. But tonight was different. She looked around the small room, decorated in shades of blue and green.

"I expected your room to be pink," she said with a smile.

"Please, I'm not a little girl anymore," Jan said, looking at the walls, the floor, anywhere but at Tina. Finally she laughed. "Okay, I gave Dad my master suite while his arm is healing because it's downstairs and has an en suite bathroom. It's rose and cream," she said with a guilty smile. "Rose sounds much more grown-up than pink."

"Oh, definitely," Tina agreed with a laugh. She edged past the bed and went over to the desk that had been placed against the far wall. She turned the chair around to sit and face Jan, their knees nearly touching in the cramped room.

"Don't try to convince me you're shy," Jan said. Her smile seemed a bit wary now. "If you don't want to be here…"

Tina reached out and captured one of Jan's hands. She kissed her knuckles, biting one gently. "Oh, I want to be here. Very much." She cradled Jan's hand in her lap. "But I don't want to rush. Why don't we just talk first?"

"Because three hours of conversation in the car wasn't enough?" Jan asked in a teasing tone. She gave Tina's hand a squeeze. "Okay. What shall we talk about?"

Tina hesitated. She wasn't sure where to begin, how to articulate her thoughts to Jan when they didn't make sense in her own mind. When the incoherent notes floating inside her didn't resemble any song she'd ever known. "I don't know," she said. Brilliant.

Jan smiled. She had been worried Tina might be regretting her decision to stay the night, had regretted not suggesting they go to an anonymous hotel instead of here, to her home and all it represented. But the feel of Tina's teeth against her fingers, the way Tina was stroking her hand and wrist, gave her confidence. Tina wanted her, too, and although she was moving slowly—whether for Jan's benefit or her own—she wasn't trying to stop. Jan had been expecting to stay passive, to let Tina take control and lead them through the night on her own terms, staying within her comfort zone. But there was an unexpected uncertainty about her, and Jan stepped up to take the lead.

"Why don't I start?" she asked. She settled on her side, propped up on one elbow while her other hand remained firm in Tina's grasp. "I'll tell you a story. About the first time I saw you and imagined us together."

She could see Tina swallow, but her expression stayed calm. "I like stories," Tina said.

"Good. So, I was in a church, at my best friend's wedding rehearsal. Hardly a proper place to be thinking about sex. But I was staring at one of the quartet members, watching her play the processional, and I couldn't help myself."

"You're only human," Tina said.

"I know," Jan continued, sighing as Tina's fingertips traced a path up her forearm. She wanted to grab Tina and kiss her. Replace words with actual contact. But she struggled to keep talking, even though every ounce of her body's attention concentrated on the area where Tina was touching her. "Anyway, she was playing with vibrato, and I swear I could feel her fingers moving over me, in me. She was biting her lip, and I could feel her teeth against my neck, my stomach…" Jan switched from the dreamy tone to her normal voice. "Unfortunately, I later found out she had slept with Brooke, so I had to change my focus to the violinist."

Tina gave her a slap on the wrist. "Amusing, but untrue. I saw you staring at me during the entire rehearsal."

"Only because you were staring back."

Tina kissed the spot she had just slapped. "Go on. Finish the story."

"Later that night, I was lying in my hotel bed and thinking about her. I wanted to call, to invite her to the hotel bar for a drink."

Tina got off her chair and moved to sit on the bed. Jan scooted up until she was lying on her back, her head resting on the pillow.

"That explains why you sounded so flustered when I suggested we meet in the bar at the Davenport."

Jan smiled. "I confess, I was remembering all the things I had imagined you doing to me. Under the table in the bar, in the elevator, the hall, my room…"

Tina braced one hand on the bed next to Jan's head. The fingers of her other hand drew lazy circles on Jan's neck. "When you were in the hotel room thinking about me, did you touch yourself?"

Jan felt a tightening in her throat. Having Tina so close yet barely touching, the intensity of words bridging the distance between them, was overwhelming. "Well, no. Brooke was in the other bed crying at the time. Very frustrating," Jan said. "But other nights, in other beds? Yes, I did."

Tina brushed her nose against Jan's, and Jan involuntarily rose slightly off the bed, reaching for Tina's lips. But Tina pulled back. "You have a real gift for this," she said. "Tell me another story. The one about the night we played pool."

"Ah, the night I beat you at pool. That's a good story."

Tina laughed again and settled on her side next to Jan, rubbing her cheek against Jan's shoulder.

"I was wet before we even got to the pool table," Jan said, finding it easier to talk without eye contact. Tina made a strangled sound and pressed closer, wrapping her arm around Jan's waist. "I watched you on stage, and I wanted you so much. I wanted to lick the sweat off your neck, wanted to feel how strong your arms were while you were leaning over me."

"I was playing for you," Tina whispered, close to her ear. The feel of her breath, as much as the words themselves, made Jan shiver. "I wasn't sure I could make it back to my seat without falling because all through the song I was picturing being with you."

"Mmm, and then the pool game," Jan continued. "You were so close behind me, but not touching."

Tina laughed and flicked her tongue along Jan's neck. "Because I couldn't stop staring at your ass," she said, sliding her hand under Jan and cupping her bottom. The combination of her tongue and hand made Jan gasp. She had never been so turned on.

Tina felt Jan shift restlessly beside her, felt the heat from between her legs as she moved her hand from Jan's ass to her thigh. She was torn by the need to start ripping off clothes and take Jan now, and the desire to keep the pace slow. She was sure Jan was as ready as she was. Her change in pace would probably be welcomed. But Tina wanted slow, wanted to build something, even if it took all night. Even if she passed out in frustration halfway through. She took a deep breath and exhaled against Jan's jawline, smiling as Jan made a whimpering sound and bit her lower lip.

"What happened next?" Tina prompted. "You came home and went to bed. To this bed?"

"Yes," Jan said, her eyes closed.

"And did you take your top off?"

"Yes," Jan repeated, a small smile on her lips as Tina rose to a sitting position.

"I need some visuals with this story, so let's try to recreate it as accurately as possible," Tina said, reaching for the hem of Jan's shirt. "No," she said when Jan started to help her. "Keep your eyes closed and let me. Just shift a little…there."

Tina tossed Jan's shirt and bra onto the floor. She waged another battle between moving fast or painfully slow as she stared at Jan's breasts, their nipples tight and rosy and so beautiful Tina thought she might cry. Slow won again, but by a much smaller margin. She permitted herself one slow stroke across Jan's chest, watching Jan arch toward her touch, before she settled her hand lightly on Jan's stomach.

"What about jeans? I remember you were wearing them at the pub, and oh my, did they fit you well. But did you take them off before you got into bed?"

Jan pressed the heel of her hand against her eyes and nodded. Tina was glad to see Jan look as tortured as she herself felt. She wouldn't be able to last much longer. She slowly unbuttoned Jan's pants, easing her fingers beyond the edge of the denim and tracing them along Jan's lower abdomen before she slid the jeans down Jan's legs. Tina could smell her arousal, could feel the damp crotch of the jeans in her hand as she resisted the urge to yank them off. She turned her attention to Jan's yellow panties, dropping a quick kiss on her mound before she slid the scrap of cotton off and dropped it on the growing pile of clothing on the floor.

"So," Tina said, keeping her words and voice calm even though she felt anything but. "You were in bed, naked. Then what?"

"You touched me, I came, the end," Jan said in a rush.

Tina laughed and rose onto her knees, straddling Jan's hips but still barely brushing against her bare skin. "Your storytelling skills are degrading," she said, licking a trail from Jan's stomach to her throat. Her hair brushed against Jan's nipples, and she felt the touch like a tangible thing.

"I won't be able to string two words together much longer," Jan said.

"Do you realize you're naked and lying beneath me, but we haven't even kissed yet?" Tina asked, her face only centimeters from Jan's.

"That somehow seems inappropriate," Jan said, her mouth curving in a smile. "Maybe you should do something about it."

"Maybe something like this?" Tina asked, pressing her lips against Jan's with gentle pressure. "Or this," she suggested as she tugged on Jan's lower lip with her teeth. "Or—"

The third time, Jan rose up and met her halfway, opening her mouth in an invitation Tina couldn't refuse. Her tongue found Jan's as she dropped onto her elbows, her weight easing down and against Jan's naked body. All of Tina's waiting, her self-control, her hesitation disappeared as she sank into Jan's welcoming kiss. Slow was no longer an option. She felt Jan's need, and it overrode her own. One arm supported her weight while the other moved between their bodies, until Tina's hand gently rested between Jan's thighs, cupping her loosely, close enough for Tina to feel how wet Jan was.

"I want…" Jan said when Tina lifted her head, breaking away from her kiss.

"I know," Tina said with a smile. Jan was so gorgeous, with her gold hair fanned out on the pillow and her eyes dark and unfocused. She slid her trembling fingers into Tina's hair and Tina leaned into the tight hold, anchoring herself to Jan. "But tell me anyway."

"Touch me, please, right there…" Jan whispered, her words punctuated with small gasps as Tina followed her commands. "Feel how wet I am for you. Yes…"

Tina groaned as Jan drew the simple word out, lengthening the one syllable as Tina slowly stroked her. "Tell me more," Tina demanded, her voice rough with desire.

"I need you in…side…Fuck, yes. Just like that," Jan whimpered as she pressed her hips against Tina's hand, guiding her as much by her actions as by her words. Tina moved in her, over her, as she matched Jan's rhythm and then gradually increased her pressure and speed until she took control of their pace. She sensed Jan trying to slow down, but instead of matching her hesitation, Tina increased the pressure of her fingers and thumb, relentlessly driving Jan toward her climax.

"Now," Tina said, holding her hand gently over Jan's mouth to muffle her cries. "Come. Now."

Jan did, biting Tina's hand as she felt her body, her muscles, her heart contract and then release in one terrifying burst of power. Tina stopped moving but stayed close, pressing firmly against Jan's clit until she shuddered once more and then sagged wearily on the bed. Tina released her, curving her damp hand around Jan's waist and resting her head on Jan's chest.

"You bit me really hard," Tina said, her voice somewhat muffled as she burrowed close. Jan wrapped both arms around her.

"Sorry," she said. "If I hadn't, I would have screamed." She laughed and then sighed as a small aftershock trembled through her body. Tina moaned quietly as if sharing the sensation.

"If I admit I kind of liked it, would I scare you off?" Tina asked.

"Not a chance," Jan said, her hands sifting through Tina's hair, starting with a slow tempo and gradually increasing the pace. She slowly registered the different textures against her overly sensitive skin. Tina's face, her soft hair, the wooly scratch of her green fisherman sweater, the rough denim jeans. "Why are you still wearing clothes?"

"No time to take them off," Tina murmured. "Couldn't stop touching you."

Jan stretched her legs and felt Tina's hips press against her. A gentle rush of power struck her as she realized how attuned Tina was to her every move. A shift of her thigh, a stroke of her fingers, a brush of her lips against Tina's hair. Tina seemed sensitive to every nuance of Jan's body, and Jan knew it wasn't because the touches were overtly sexual or demanding, but because Jan's own arousal and release had built up this energy in Tina's body. Tina had been turned on by touching *her*, and the simple knowledge was thrilling to Jan.

She loosened her hold. "Get undressed," she said. Tina sat up and gave her a quick kiss before she stood, her back to Jan, and started to pull her sweater over her head.

"Wait." Jan got off the bed and came to stand behind Tina. She wrapped her arms around Tina's middle, gently disengaging her hands from the sweater's hem.

"Please don't tell me you're changing your mind *now*," Tina said in a low voice laced with desire and impatience.

Jan laughed. "Of course not." She felt Tina relax into her embrace. "Why the boardwalk?" she asked.

"What?"

"Why did you pick the boardwalk as the place of our fictional first kiss? Was it the first time you felt attracted to me?"

"No way. I thought you were beautiful and sexy when I first saw you at the rehearsal. And when we met for drinks in the Peacock Room. And definitely in the pub, when you were leaning over the pool table. I wanted to take you right then."

"So," Jan said, grinding her hips against Tina's ass. "Back to my original question. Why'd you choose the pier?"

Tina dropped her head back onto Jan's shoulder. Jan kissed her neck, adding a flick of her tongue. "Mmm," Tina moaned. "I guess because we hugged. And argued. And laughed." She gave a sharp intake of breath between each brief sentence as Jan continued to kiss her neck. "I was attracted to you from the start, but that was the day I knew I could…trust you. Before then, you could have had my body anytime, but from that day on, you could have had more."

Jan nibbled on the tight tendon at the base of Tina's neck. She knew Tina wasn't professing her undying love. She wasn't offering anything beyond this single agreed-upon night together. But she was giving Jan more than a disinterested sexual fling. Friendship, connection, communication. Jan recognized the gift for what it was. No more, no less.

"And you wouldn't have pushed me away if I had, say, slipped my hand under your shirt when I was holding you, out there by the lake?" Jan rubbed her hand over Tina's tight abdomen and up to cup her breast, using her thumb and forefinger to knead an already-erect nipple. "Even though we were in public, and anyone could have seen us?"

"I think it would have been perfectly acceptable," Tina said, pushing her chest into Jan's hand. Jan moved her hand across to Tina's other breast, sliding under her bra. Jan closed her hand, firmly massaging Tina's breast. "Besides, who could even tell what you're… oh God, yes…doing?"

Jan's nipples tightened in response to the friction of Tina's sweater as Tina moved against her. Jan felt her whole body vibrate with excitement as Tina squirmed, her words punctuated by small whimpers, her arousal obviously increasing.

Jan hooked the thumb of her free hand in the top of Tina's jeans. "What if I had unbuttoned your jeans so I could reach my hand inside and touch you? Would they have been able to tell what I was doing, then?"

Jan moved her hand to Tina's crotch and squeezed gently. She rubbed against the hot, soaked denim and whispered in Tina's ear. "Would you have cared if anyone saw?"

Tina laughed, a rough, weak laugh. "Not even a tiny bit."

Jan brought her hand up to Tina's chin and turned her so they were facing each other. The smell of Tina on her hand made her ache to touch her, taste her, take her. "What if I had gotten on my knees right there on the boardwalk and sucked you until you came in my mouth? Would you have tried to stop me?"

Tina shook her head, leaning forward to kiss Jan. Hungry, searching. "Please," she whispered. "Make me come."

Jan unbuttoned Tina's jeans, keeping eye contact until she had them open. Then she dropped to her knees, shoving the intrusive material out of her way, off Tina's hips. She used her thumbs to spread Tina open and slid her tongue through the inviting wetness. They both groaned at her gentle touch, and Jan couldn't tell where her voice left off and Tina's began. She licked harder, deeper, until she felt Tina's thighs tremble beneath her hands. Then she circled Tina's clit with her tongue before closing her lips around it and sucking. She felt Tina jerk against her face, felt Tina's hands tangled in her hair, felt a concordant rush of wetness on her own thighs.

❖

About an hour later, Tina rested in the hazy moonlight, Jan's head pillowed on her chest. She wanted to wake Jan to fuck her again. And again. But she let her sleep, running her fingers from Jan's temple to the ends of her hair, over and over, as she synchronized her breathing with the tempo of Jan's heartbeat.

Tina smiled in the semidarkness as she remembered scenes from the night, whispered words, revealed fantasies. She had figured she'd enjoy being with Jan in bed. Jan had a great body, and she carried herself with a sexy confidence. Besides, Tina had never had cause to doubt her own ability to lead her partner through a mutually satisfying experience. But being with Jan had been unexpected. Different. Amazing.

Tina massaged Jan's scalp gently before slipping her hands through the pliant strands. Maybe it was the talking. She usually limited herself to necessary words during sex, like *right there*, *harder*, and *yes*. But the joking, the shared memories, the vulnerability of combining words and touch and emotion were things Tina had never experienced before. Probably because she rarely knew a woman well enough to carry on such an extended conversation. Or because she had never cared to know one so well.

Jan sighed and curled closer. Tina traced one finger over the small dove tattooed on Jan's shoulder. No matter how wonderful, how intimate the night had been, the cold facts of day were unchanged. Jan was searching for safety and stability. For a home, for the strength needed to bear the responsibility of holding a steady job and caring for her father. Tina wanted…well, she wasn't quite sure. But she wouldn't accept less than complete freedom. The opportunity to work, love, and live according to her own desires. Meaning no family obligations—whether hers or a partner's—no ties binding her to place or boss or girlfriend.

Tina rubbed her cheek against Jan's head. Of course, she had to make money and cultivate clients, so she needed some stability in her work life. Especially if she accepted more of the extended PR projects she found so interesting and fulfilling. And while she was free to move anywhere, she had always stayed in Seattle where she had a base of friends and hobbies and companionship. But she could move anywhere she wanted.

Even Spokane? She dismissed the question as soon as she asked it. No. Of course, it was feasible to do her type of work from here, with occasional trips to Seattle. But what did she really have in this city? Some family, perhaps, but they looked better from a distance. Jan? Tina closed her eyes and pressed her lips against Jan's hair. How could she even consider making plans for the future, settling, tying herself down? Just a foolish side effect of lovemaking. Yes, their connection had been something special, something unique, but how long would it last? Not long, if it even still existed now that the first haze of passion had cleared. From this point on, sex with Jan would probably only offer the exciting—but expected—physical satisfaction Tina was accustomed to feeling.

Tina's hand slid from the tattoo, over Jan's shoulder, and down to cup her breast. Might as well test her theory and have some boring, predictable sex. She rubbed her palm over Jan's nipple and was rewarded by an intake of breath and the feeling of Jan tightening against her like a bowstring. Tina's touch grew more insistent as her own breathing quickened. Jan stirred, fully awake now, and raised her head. When their lips met, something exploded inside of Tina. The kiss was at once calming and erotic, familiar and fiery. Just a kiss. How could it mean so much? Tina broke their contact and moved down Jan's body. She needed passion and climax and mindless sex. Anything to silence the frightening thoughts running through her mind.

Chapter Thirteen

Tina, wake up." Jan pulled on a T-shirt before returning to the bed to shake a sleeping Tina by the shoulder. She went to the closet and grabbed a pair of worn khakis, hopping toward the bed on one foot as she hurried into the pants. She shook Tina again. Harder. She should have woken hours earlier and sent Tina home, so their fantasy night didn't intrude on real life. She couldn't risk letting Tina fill her home, her daily routine, with color and smell and laughter any more than she already had. Life was already going to be drab and empty when she was gone.

"Wake up!"

Tina startled her by snaking out a hand and taking hold of Jan's wrist. Jan was off balance enough to tumble onto the bed when Tina tugged.

"Mmm," Tina mumbled in a sexy, sleepy voice. "You sound cranky, but you look beautiful. Let's sleep a little longer." She burrowed under the covers again, keeping her arms wrapped tightly around Jan. Jan sighed and relaxed for one brief moment. She felt so comfortable snuggled close to Tina. Too damned comfortable. She wriggled and finally managed to pull herself out of Tina's embrace. She got out of bed.

"Tina, you have to get up. It's getting late."

Her whisper must have sounded agitated enough to rouse Tina. She sat up in bed and rubbed her eyes. "It's dark outside," she said. "What time is it?"

"Five o'clock."

"In the morning?"

"Of course in the morning."

"Huh," Tina said, pulling up her knees and clasping her arms around them. "I've heard rumors such a time existed, but I didn't really believe them until now."

Tina looked drowsy and tousled and good enough to eat. Jan shook her head. Sex with Tina had been a fun diversion, but their relationship wouldn't last in the harsh daylight of reality. The longer they dragged out their good-byes, the harder they'd be. Jan already felt more raw pain than she had expected. Tina would take a piece of Jan with her when she left, leaving her feeling shapeless. Undefined. She had tried to be cautious, to be prepared for the morning after. But she hadn't expected the night before to be so fucking incredible.

"Get up and get dressed," Jan ordered.

"Where are we going so early?" Tina yawned and dangled her legs over the side of the bed.

"We're not going anywhere. *You* need to go before my dad wakes up."

"You're kidding," Tina said with a laugh. Her smile faded when Jan didn't answer. "Really?"

"Yes." Jan was resolute. She handed Tina her sweater. One more minute, one more second, and she'd be back in bed with her. Tina had claimed every part of Jan she had touched. Pretty soon, there wouldn't be anything left of her. Tina had been an exciting sex partner, just as Jan had predicted, but she would never be the real partner Jan needed.

"Don't be silly," Tina said, but she pulled her sweater over her head. "First of all, you're not a teenager, and second, your dad likes me. I doubt he'll care I stayed the night. I thought the three of us could go out to breakfast again. I feel like a huge chicken-fried steak and some fried eggs."

"Let me put it this way," Jan said slowly. She couldn't face a happy family breakfast. Tina had already become too much a part of Jan's bed, her room, her life. "I *want* you to go before my dad gets up."

Tina stood up and gently cupped her hands around Jan's chin. "You're serious, aren't you? But why? I thought last night was…well, something special."

Jan took hold of Tina's wrists and pulled her hands away. Something special. Last night had been fun, an extension of her playful relationship with Tina, a chance to live out some of her fantasies. But Tina hadn't been just the lover she had fantasized about. She had been too much more. Her body felt pleasantly sore and satisfied after a night of sex, but her heart felt chafed and aching. The laughter and play and lightness had somehow burrowed into her, more deeply and intimately than Jan had anticipated.

"The sex was great," she said. "But we all know how this story ends. You're leaving Spokane soon, and even if you weren't, a relationship isn't your style. Let's call it a fun night and let it go at that."

"Okay, okay," Tina said. She picked up the jeans she had tossed on the floor the night before and pulled them on. "No breakfast. But can we meet later? Get some coffee and talk this out?"

"Talk what out?" Jan asked, her voice rising above a whisper as her pain and frustration fused into anger. "Our whole relationship has been a game. Pretend, make-believe, fantasy. But my life isn't any of those things. And don't try to tell me you plan to stick around after the game ends. It's not your style."

"Maybe it hasn't been my style in the past. But people change. I might not be exactly the girlfriend you planned for, but—"

"How could you be anyone's girlfriend?" Jan snapped, her voice no longer confined to a whisper. Because, damn it, she wanted Tina to be the kind of woman she could depend on, count on. "The term suggests some sort of commitment, and you'll have none of that. In and out, unpredictable, no desire to be tied down."

"Shallow, unreliable, uncaring," Tina added.

Jan might have chosen those adjectives before she had gotten to know Tina, but no longer. Still, if it helped her get Tina out the door faster..."Your words, not mine," she said, with an indifferent shrug.

"I suppose that's all a rigid and narrow-minded person like you would see in me. You have your inflexible life all planned out, and you won't make any changes to accommodate someone who isn't precisely the right shape. But just because I don't fit the ideal doesn't mean we wouldn't be good together."

"Good together for what? Another night? Maybe a week?" Jan asked. She felt a stubborn urge to argue against the word *rigid*, but she couldn't deny its accuracy. But how could it be wrong to stay firm and uncompromising when it came to such an important issue as love? "And even though they aren't right for you, you can't convince me stability and security and trust are bad things."

"You know you can trust me," Tina said in a frighteningly low voice.

Of course she could. But Jan had to push forward. Tina was almost gone. "I can trust you to *leave* me eventually. So just go now and don't drag it out. You'll be running away from your family again soon enough, and when you do, you'll leave me behind, too. I'd rather get it over with now, so I can go back to my real world."

Tina clenched her hands into fists. She had been trying to explain to Jan how she felt, how much she wanted to—for once in her life—stick around to see if they could strengthen the temporary bonds they had made during the night. She understood Jan being concerned about her long list of past lovers, but bringing her family into the mess was too much. "I *never* ran away from my family. *They* abandoned me and my mom after Dad died. And when Mom was sick, I was left all alone to take care of her."

"No," Jan said. "*I* am all alone. From what Peter has said, and what you yourself admitted, you had offers of help but you turned them down because you were still angry over stupid fights from your childhood. Right now, I'd give anything to have the kind of support you have."

"Careful what you wish for. That support comes with way too many strings." Tina was furious. How could Jan misinterpret her, her family, her past so badly? "I'd rather have my freedom than any help from them."

"Oh, right. Your precious freedom. But ask yourself, do you really want to be free, or do you want to be alone? Because you carry your family, your past with you everywhere you go. You say you don't want to be tied down or confined by obligations, but you wear your anger and resentment like chains."

"And you claim to want a real home with people who care about you, but you refuse to let anyone close enough to intrude on your self-pitying solitude," Tina said as she picked up her keys and shoes. She had thought Jan was the one person who had been able to really understand her, to see past her fear of getting close to someone, only to lose them. She had been wrong. She paused before opening the door. "And don't insult your dad by pretending you didn't have any stability in your life. The background might have changed a lot, but the love and security he gave you never did. Sometime, ask him what sacrifice he made for that to happen."

❖

Jan slowly trailed down the stairs after Tina. She knew she had damaged their friendship beyond repair, and even if she had wanted to call her back, to try to make amends, Tina would never forgive her. Bringing Tina's relationship with her family into the fight had been unacceptable, and although Jan firmly believed she was correct about Tina being bound by her anger, she never should have brought it up in the heat of an argument. But Jan had been too angry herself—and too hurt—to stop.

"Good morning, pumpkin," her dad said when she entered the kitchen. He was struggling with the top of a milk carton he had braced against his sling. Jan took it from him and opened it.

"Thanks," he said, pouring some into a measuring cup.

"How much did you hear?" she asked.

"Just voices, no words. Are you okay?"

Jan sniffed and nodded. "It's for the best."

"Whatever you say. I thought you might want some of my famous blueberry pancakes. They always cheered you up when you were little."

Jan smiled. Memories of skinned knees, elementary-school traumas, and lost toys—all made better by a big stack of pancakes and syrup—played through her mind. This problem was too big to be fixed by a sugar high, but the batter *did* smell good. "Can I help?" she asked.

Her dad emptied a pint of fresh berries into the bowl. "You could get the frying pan off the shelf for me," he suggested. She gave him a teary kiss on the cheek and went over to the cupboard.

"Tina said something about you making sacrifices for me when I was a kid," she said as she carried the heavy pan to the island in the middle of the kitchen. "Do you know what she meant?"

"Choices, not sacrifices," her dad said. "But I suppose we shouldn't put off talks any longer, should we. Why don't we talk about it over breakfast?"

CHAPTER FOURTEEN

"You look like hell," Peter said. He wedged past a boisterous group of kids wearing Gonzaga shirts and sat on the red vinyl-covered stool next to Tina.

"Gee, thanks," she said. She was sure he was telling the truth, but she'd been avoiding looking in mirrors since her fight with Jan. The dark circles under her eyes and the frown lines curving around her mouth only reminded her of how different she felt now than she had when she'd first woken up in Jan's bed. Then, she had been exhausted after making love all night but had been unable to stop smiling. Now, she felt and looked—as Peter had so politely phrased it—like hell.

"This place makes a great burger, but it doesn't offer much in the way of privacy," Peter said, "You said you needed to talk. We could go somewhere quieter."

"This is fine," Tina said, moving out of the way as one of the college boys gestured wildly and nearly hit her in the head. The dive, crammed on a corner lot, was tiny and only had room for an L-shaped Formica counter that wrapped around its questionable-looking grill. But Brooke and Jan had raved about it, recounting a series of stories about eating here when they were students at Gonzaga. This was the place they had originally planned to visit for lunch the day they had driven to Wenatchee instead. Tina wondered if she and Jan still would have spent the night together if they'd stuck to their original idea. Or had the challenge of adapting to a reformulated plan been the catalyst for Jan's suggestion they spend the night together? The day had been out of the ordinary, so why not the night as well?

"Double cheeseburger, onion rings, and a cherry malt, please," Tina said, when the kid who was acting as fry cook came over to take their order. Apparently, he performed every job in the place.

"Ugh, how can you eat all that?" Peter asked. He sighed and put the paper menu back in its metal holder. "Same for me. And I hope you have a cardiologist on call. Now, what's up?"

Tina watched their waiter dump a pile of onion rings into a vat of oil. She doubted it had been cleaned since Jan had been a freshman in college. "How do you remember our childhood?" she finally asked. "I mean, the times when my parents and I would come visit."

Peter hesitated. "I don't think my memories are as bad as yours," he said, sounding as if he was treading cautiously.

Cautious or not, Tina felt her anger simmer. Rage seemed so close to the surface these days. "Are you saying I just imagined all the fights? The bitterness?"

"Oh, I think the bitterness is very real," he said. He nudged her with his elbow. "A joke. Sorry. And no, I don't think everything was perfect."

"Not perfect," Tina said with a snort. "There's an understatement."

"But it also wasn't as bad as you remember," he said. "I guess I had a different perspective. First, my dad stayed here in Spokane while yours moved away, so Gran wasn't angry with him. Most of the time, she seemed like a fairly normal grandmother. Never affectionate, but at least not hostile."

"What an accomplishment. She should have it engraved on her Grandmother of the Year trophy."

"Second," Peter continued as if he hadn't heard her. "You were a child. You were caught in the middle of a very emotional situation, and you couldn't understand any of the subtext. I grew up around the family, so eventually I was either told or I figured out what was going on in the background, what emotions made Gran lash out in anger."

Tina had a sudden vision of her and Jan arguing. Jan's words had stung, but Tina had been able to see Jan's pain and fear behind them. Jan just hadn't trusted her enough to let her get close, to give Tina a chance to prove herself. "So, please tell me, what excuses did Gran give you for yelling at my mom?"

"No excuses," Peter said. He paused while the cook set their food on the counter. "But my dad, Gran, everyone—they loved your father. Uncle Pete was always the favorite in the family. He moved away soon after our grandfather died, and Gran was very upset. She had a lot of built-up resentment because she had never wanted to move to the States in the first place, and I think she felt abandoned when she lost both of the men she loved in one year. She was probably angry with your dad, but no one ever seemed to get mad at him, so Gran took it out on your mom, instead. He was caught in the middle."

"Not just on my mom," Tina said. She yanked a straw out of its paper sleeve and stuffed it through the plastic lid on her malt. "She had plenty to say about me, too."

Peter took a huge bite of his burger and wiped ketchup off his chin. "Well, you were a horrible little brat."

Tina stared at him. "How dare you. Do I need to kick your ass? Because I can, you know."

Peter groaned as he shoved an onion ring in his mouth. "Believe me, I haven't forgotten," he said dramatically. "Okay, you win. You were a perfect little angel." He paused, and then gave a snort of laughter. "But remember the snake incident? Gran still won't get her own mail out of the box. She picks it up at the post office."

Tina laughed along with him and took a bite of her burger, suddenly feeling hungry. "Thank God, Lindsay was there, so we could blame her. Not that she'd ever have been brave enough to pick up a snake. You weren't either, as I recall."

"You were something," Peter said. "Never afraid of anything."

Tina wiped grease off her fingers with a paper napkin. She had been brave back then. But the transition from wild child to adult, after her dad died and her mom was diagnosed, had been too abrupt to handle, without replacing some of the bravery with caution. She had learned how to protect herself.

Peter lifted his paper cup and tapped it against hers. "But we've had a chance to get to know one another again, and I'm glad about that."

"Me, too," she said, without reservation. "I know Dad would be happy about it, too. He probably would have dragged us to Spokane every damned year if he hadn't died. Maybe, eventually, he would have forced us to get along through sheer stubbornness."

"Yeah, Dad always said Uncle Pete was as mule headed as Gran." He patted her on the arm. "Luckily, the trait skipped a generation and left you so tractable."

Tina swiped one of his onion rings. "Hilarious. But thanks," she said, sobering a little. "For talking this out with me. I might have liked seeing you and Lindsay more as we got older, but Mom really didn't want anything to do with the family after we lost Dad."

"That's not quite true," Peter said, his voice soft. "She and my dad communicated quite often. She had a lawyer in Seattle, but she turned to him for legal advice all the time. That's how Gran knew when she needed hospice care, and why she contacted you about helping pay for it."

Tina stared at him. "But why didn't Mom…"

He patted her arm awkwardly. "She was making preparations, writing her will…She probably didn't want to upset you."

After a pause, Peter started talking about some of the handmade planters he had ordered for his new farmers' market booth. Tina listened as he talked, adding her advice for how to market the artisanal products, but part of her mind was preoccupied. Traveling back in time and reevaluating what she'd seen through the eyes of a child.

❖

Jan leaned on her desk and watched her student struggle through a theorem at the whiteboard. It was always a challenge to keep the kids interested in math and learning, but the last two weeks of school were especially trying. Polygons and postulates couldn't compete with prom and graduation and the lure of summer breezes just outside the window. But she could barely keep her mind focused on work, so she couldn't fault the restless teenagers for their inattentiveness.

She finally gave up the pretense of teaching and told her class to study quietly for the last five minutes, until the bell rang. While they pretended to read their textbooks, she sat at her desk and pretended to write something of great importance. They were actually whispering and passing notes—clearly not geometry-related, and she sketched a series of interlocking hexagons on a piece of paper—clearly not important at all. Shapes and forms. They had always seemed so comforting to her. Well-defined. Easily measured. Even the shapes on a woman's body attracted her. Circles and triangles, begging to be traced and studied and appreciated. Jan's first impressions of Tina had been defined by the planes and angles of her face, the proportions of her measurements. But the simple, clear shape of Tina had changed, had gained dimension and depth, and suddenly there was more to her—more complexity and variability—than Jan could handle.

The bell finally rang, and Jan dismissed her class. She headed to the break room and aimed for the coffeepot. She needed a caffeine boost if she hoped to make it through her next few classes. Chloe was sitting in the corner of the room, at a small round table, and Jan took her heavily sweetened coffee and joined her.

"Mind if I sit?" she asked. Chloe was reading, and she started when Jan spoke. She blushed and quickly stuffed the magazine in her briefcase, but not before Jan saw a picture of a bride on the glossy cover.

"Oh my God! Are you engaged?"

Chloe shushed her and glanced around the room. It was empty except for the two of them.

"No one else is here, so I think we're safe," Jan said with a laugh. "So, did Peter propose?"

"Not yet," Chloe admitted. "But he's been acting strangely, and I think he's planning something. But, please, don't say anything in case I'm misreading him."

"He won't hear a word from me," Jan promised. Tina might claim she didn't want any ties or obligations to others, but she had somehow managed to snare Jan in a web of relations. A growing friendship with Chloe, more contact with Andy and Brooke, a sense of belonging with Peter and his musical friends. But her only real connection to Peter was through Tina, so she doubted she'd be seeing him much, from now on.

Chloe went on to prove her wrong. "If he does ask me, I'd want you…I mean if you wouldn't mind…to be my maid of honor."

Jan stared at her. "Me?" she finally asked. She liked Chloe, but she was surprised by the request. "I'd be glad to, of course, but if you're only asking because I was there when you met—"

"Jan, I'm asking because you're my closest friend," Chloe said with a shake of her head.

"I am?" Jan blurted out. She realized too late how rude the words sounded, but Chloe laughed.

"I hate to break it to you, but yes. I didn't know anyone in Spokane when I took this job, and you've been so nice to me."

"Well then, I'd be honored. Sorry to sound surprised." Jan struggled to explain her reaction. "I moved around a lot before I settled here, so I'm not used to having close friends. I guess I learned to keep my distance because I was always expecting to move away."

"Tough, isn't it?" Chloe asked. "We moved a few times while I was growing up. It was hard to make new friends, but I loved reading, so the first thing my parents did every time we moved to a new city was get me a library card. It made me feel at home."

"My dad signed me up for art classes whenever he could. I liked sculpture, especially. Forming things with my hands."

"It's easier to carry books from place to place than pieces of sculpture," Chloe said with a laugh.

Jan thought back to the careful way her dad packed every piece she had made. He still had them and had insisted on bringing them when he moved into her house. The prints of fighter planes had been left hanging on the apartment walls, but her naïve artwork covered every surface in the rose-colored room. "You're right. Dad spent a fortune on Bubble Wrap over the years."

"How is he doing?" Chloe asked, her voice soft. After her dad's last appointment with the doctor, Jan had finally confided in Chloe about his prognosis. She was relieved she had, since she no longer had Tina as confidante.

"He's well, thanks. It'll be nice to have the summer together. I've been planning lots of day trips for us."

"Just be sure to take some time out for you, too," Chloe said. "Peter and I are happy to check in on him, anytime. Actually, Peter was really touched when Tina asked him to help the other day."

"When Tina asked…what?"

"When you went to the bluegrass festival. Tina gave your dad Peter's number in case he needed someone to call while you were out of town. I thought you knew. Did you have fun?"

Chloe glossed over Tina's act as if it wasn't a big deal, but Jan was overwhelmed by Tina's effort to take care of her and her dad. Such a small gesture, but it had a huge impact on her ability to breathe. She winced when she remembered calling Tina untrustworthy.

"Um, it was fun," she said. The festival was a blur to her now. The night after? So vividly etched in her mind, she could scarcely go a minute without recalling some part of it. She had fought hard to keep from going, from changing plans at the last minute, from being spontaneous and adventurous instead of…What had Tina called her? Oh, yes, rigid and inflexible. Jan sighed. She missed Tina, but she had to be realistic. The novelty of helping Jan and her dad would have worn off soon, and Tina would have inevitably left. At least, the Tina Jan imagined she knew—the shallow playgirl—would have left. The real Tina was proving to be much more complex.

"So, show me your magazine," Jan said, desperate to change the subject. "And, please, tell me I don't have to wear a big frilly dress."

Chapter Fifteen

Tina closed her computer program and rubbed a hand wearily over her eyes. Thursday night. She had spent too many hours staring at the screen, watching images from Jan's life flash in front of her as she finished editing Glen's DVD. She knew she was only torturing herself as she played the movie over and over, but the small thrill she felt when she saw Jan's face, her smile, was worth the pain when reality hit, yet again. She had opened up to Jan, offering to try for more of a relationship than her usual weekend flings, but Jan wasn't interested. She refused to look past Tina's reputation, past the surface charm Tina wore too easily, and see the real person inside. Tina didn't fit Jan's preplanned idea of a partner, and she refused to make any effort to modify her expectations. Tina knew, deep down, that what they could have had together would have far surpassed any perfect relationship Jan had imagined. Tina believed she and Jan would have made a great team, dealing with the messy past and complicated future together.

But Jan didn't agree, and Tina was left alone to deal with the present. Including her family. Part of the reason she had stayed so engrossed in editing was to keep her mind off tonight's celebration of Peter's birthday. A big party would have been manageable, but an intimate dinner with close relatives was a frightening prospect. And if she didn't hurry, she wouldn't be on time. Her grandmother would probably love a chance to criticize her tardiness, and Tina was tempted to arrive late just to antagonize her, but tonight was about Peter, not about her own issues. So she hurried into black jeans and a forest-green blouse, grabbed her violin and small amp, and pushed the speed limit through Spokane's residential streets.

"Tina! Right on time," Uncle Nick said as he opened the door and hugged her with one arm, while he tugged the amp out of her hand with the other. "I'm glad you brought the fiddle, so we can have a little family jam session later. Just like old times."

He cleared his throat and turned away from her, leading the way into the living room. She knew he meant her father when he talked about old times. She had been too young to play much when she had visited as a child. A wave of unanticipated sadness came over her as she followed him down the so-familiar hall. She had never come here alone before, and the influx of memories made her miss her parents. For a second, she wished Jan were with her, holding her hand and giving her a reassuring squeeze. But Tina could handle this alone. She had no other choice.

Nick set her amp in a corner of the room, and Tina followed with her instrument case. She said a stiff hello to her grandmother and greeted Peter and Chloe, before her Aunt Miriam came out of the kitchen and enveloped her in a tight, cinnamon-scented hug.

"It's so good to have you in our home again," Miriam said when she finally let go and Tina could breathe again.

"It's…nice to be here," Tina said awkwardly. She inhaled again. Nutmeg, warm spices, cream cheese, such familiar scents. "Do I smell gingerbread?" she asked.

"You remembered," Miriam said with a catch in her voice, giving Tina another hug. "Every birthday, every holiday, it's the only dessert I'm allowed to make. I have books full of recipes, but God forbid I suggest something different."

"And she stopped trying after the chocolate cake fiasco of 1998," Peter said, ducking as his mom snapped him with her towel.

"Let's go out to the patio, I think the grill should be ready," Miriam said. "Get Tina a drink, dear."

"I suppose you've grown out of juice in sippy cups, haven't you?" Nick asked with a laugh once the others went outside and left the two alone.

"As long as it has vodka in it, I'm still fine with juice," Tina said. "But I'd prefer whiskey on the rocks."

He dropped several cubes of ice in a glass. "I mentioned the work you've been doing for Peter to a few of my friends," he said as he poured her a generous drink. "I hope you don't mind, but a couple of them wanted to see more, and I showed them the ads you've created."

She took the drink when he offered it to her. He didn't seem inclined to rush out and join the others, so she leaned her elbow on the bar and took a sip of whiskey. "Of course I don't mind." She hesitated, wanting to seem indifferent about anyone else's opinion but curious to hear, at the same time. The scope of this project had been new and challenging for her, especially since she'd been juggling the turmoil of her relationship with Jan at the same time, but she had loved the work. She hoped the end product was as professionally successful as it had been personally satisfying. "What'd they think?" she asked in a casual voice.

Nick patted her on the shoulder. "They were both very impressed. With your use of colors and visuals, but also with your ability to carry a theme and a concept throughout the whole campaign." He paused. "I know you're almost finished with Peter's project, and you'll probably be heading back to Seattle soon. But if you decide to stay in Spokane longer, I could put you in touch with some good contacts. I'm sure you'd have as much work as you could handle."

"Wow, thanks Uncle Nick," Tina said. "I'm not sure what my plans are yet, but I'll let you know." She followed him out to the patio, stunned by her equivocation. A month ago, she would have vehemently refused to consider staying in Spokane even a second longer than necessary, and now she was struck by her desire to meet with Nick's friends. Only because she was flattered to have her work appreciated, of course. And maybe, just a little, because she had enjoyed rediscovering Peter and most of her family.

But she knew the real reason she wanted to stay was the one factor that would make it impossible to do so. She wanted to be near Jan, to hold on to the hope of a future with her. But staying in Spokane without being with Jan would be unbearable.

Even sitting at this dinner without Jan was painful. Every conversation seemed to bring her sharply to Tina's mind. She was seated between Peter and Chloe, and Tina recognized their attempt to shield her from her grandmother, but being with the two of them reminded Tina of the night they first met. And when they started talking about the time they all went to Coeur d'Alene, Tina couldn't clearly recall the actual trip, just her late-night reenactment with Jan. All her traitorous mind would dredge up were memories of Jan standing behind her, whispering Tina's fantasies in her ear. Jan's arms around her, touching and exploring. Jan on her knees, making Tina lose her mind.

Somehow, she managed to eat enough to be polite. She appreciated the casual, picnic-style meal, so different from the more formal holiday dinners she remembered. Still, she felt anxious for the evening to end, for the chance to go back to the apartment and be alone. Unfortunately, a quick getaway didn't seem to be possible.

"How about some music?" Peter suggested after they had gorged on cake. Tina had surprised herself by eating two large pieces. She had expected the childhood associations of the smell and taste of the cake to remind her of bad times, but instead, there was a comforting familiarity about it.

"I'll take care of the dishes," Chloe suggested. "The rest of you can get ready to play."

Tina licked the last bit of cream-cheese frosting off her fork, and then she offered to help Chloe stack plates and carry them to the kitchen.

"How is…" Tina wanted to ask about Jan once she and Chloe were alone, but she stopped herself. "School?" she finished.

Chloe shrugged. "She seems okay, but you know she doesn't share a lot of what she's feeling. To be honest, she looks very worn-out, but it might just be worry about her dad."

Tina rinsed a plate and handed it to Chloe to stack in the dishwasher. "I didn't ask—"

"Oh, sorry, I misunderstood," Chloe said with a smile as she busied herself rearranging plates. "School's fine. So, did you bring the electric violin you played at O'Boyle's? The one Jan called…oops, never mind. I'm sure you don't want to hear that, either."

Tina hastily dried her hands on a towel and chased after Chloe. She caught her by the elbow before she made it to the living room. "What did she say about my fiddle?"

"She said it was painted fuck-me red," Chloe whispered before pulling her arm free and leaving a stunned Tina in the doorway. Great. How could she possibly concentrate on playing *now*?

She went into the room. Nick was at the piano, playing scales as a warm-up, while Miriam polished her clarinet with a yellow cloth. Peter had set up Tina's amp but had wisely left her violin alone. She took out her glossy red fiddle and attached her shoulder rest, ignoring Chloe's smug smile. More pictures of Jan crowded into Tina's mind. At the pub, by the pool table. Tina doubted she could even play a simple C major scale if asked.

"If I'd been thinking, I'd have suggested we prepare the Bartók trio," Nick said, twisting away from the piano to face Miriam. "It was always his…a favorite."

He cleared his throat and turned back to his scales too quickly. Tina saw her grandmother stiffen. "I think I'll lie down for a bit," Francine said, leaving the room without another word.

Tina sighed. The room was getting awfully crowded with people who weren't there. Too many memories, too many unspoken thoughts. So much for a fun family music session. Of course, Tina's family wasn't exactly known for lighthearted parties.

Miriam seemed just as aware of the awkward atmosphere. "No sense pretending you don't miss your brother," she said to Nick. "We all do. So let's honor him first, and then we can move forward. Play 'Danny Boy.'"

Oh God. Tina didn't want to hear it, didn't want to play it. Her dad and grandfather had loved the simple song, had played it together hundreds of times. She had to get out of the room, out of the house, even if it meant leaving her violin behind. Peter reached across the sofa and put his hand on her arm. Damn him. How many times in the past weeks had he kept her from running away? Made her stay and share her grief, her pain, her anger, instead of going off to handle it on her own?

She sat, unmoving, while Nick played the first verse. Then, as if in a trance, she brought her fiddle to her shoulder and quietly joined him with a descant, playing an improvised embellished version of the melody an octave above the piano's voice. Miriam and Peter stayed silent while Tina and Nick played through the third verse before ending the song.

With his customary tact, Peter eventually broke the silence by strumming an opening chord on his mandolin and starting to play "Scarborough Fair." Tina smiled. Something simple and familiar, to ease the tension and move them forward. Tina picked up her violin again and played along. Somewhere in the middle of the string of English tunes, her grandmother reentered the room. Tina wondered if she had been out of earshot, or if she had just needed privacy while she listened. She shrugged off the question and focused on the music.

"One more song," Nick said eventually, barely stifling a yawn. "Tina, you pick this time."

She thought for a moment and then smiled as she started playing in the harmonic minor of a Romany tune her grandfather had taught her. She had loved to hear him play Gypsy songs, with their rapidly increasing speeds.

"I sense a challenge," Nick said as he joined in the slow refrain. On the second play through, Tina doubled her tempo.

Miriam dropped out after the first increase in speed, and Nick made it partway through the second. Tina and Peter battled it out for another round. She had to drop her grace notes and trills, sticking with the straightforward melody in her effort to play faster. Peter made it nearly to the end of the fourth round, but he hit a sour note and threw up his hands in surrender.

Tina, playing alone, finished the song with a flourish. She laughed at Peter's expression. She had won tonight, but she knew she'd better be prepared the next time. He didn't have the expression of a good loser.

"I need to practice my fingering so I can beat you," he said. "I want a rematch at Mom's birthday party."

"You're on," Tina said with a laugh before she realized what she had promised. Miriam's birthday was in September. Well, maybe she could manage to visit on occasion. If it didn't hurt too much to be close to Jan and not see her.

She busied herself with packing up her instrument, to keep her thoughts off a probable future without Jan in it, and stood to leave. She hugged her aunt and uncle, and finally turned to her grandmother.

"'Bye," Tina said, intending to keep her good-bye as quick and painless as possible. Her grandmother put her hand on Tina's elbow before she could escape.

"You play just like him," Francine said. "Like your father."

"Thank you," Tina said, surprised by what she recognized as a compliment and embarrassed as the rest of the family watched the exchange.

"Do you still have his violin?"

"It's at home," Tina answered, feeling her defenses rising again. She had the ridiculous idea her grandmother might try to get the violin back, but Tina would never let it go. She loved her fancy electric fiddle, but the acoustic instrument, her heirloom, was precious to her. "I left it with a friend for safekeeping since I didn't know where I'd be staying. I didn't want to risk damaging it." She stopped, aware that she was giving too detailed an answer to a simple question.

"I would like to hear you play it sometime," Francine said before she turned and walked away.

"I guess my audience with the queen is over," Tina muttered under her breath. Peter laughed gently as he picked up her amp and walked with her to the door.

"See? No shouting," he said.

"Dear diary..." she said dramatically. "Seriously, Peter, it was okay, but I can't even call it a good start. Grandmother and I will probably never be more comfortable around each other than this."

He shrugged and put his arm over her shoulders. "This is enough. Civility. As long as it gives you a chance to be closer to me, to Mom and Dad."

Tina couldn't argue. She had enjoyed spending time with the rest of the family. Free from some of the resentment she had carried so long.

"I'm glad you came," Peter continued as he helped her stow her gear in the car. "And thanks for my present. It's beautiful, and it sure was comfortable while I was playing."

Tina smiled. She and Jan had spent an hour searching for a gift for him at the bluegrass festival, finally discovering a colorful handwoven mandolin strap.

"Jan picked it out," she admitted. She looked down at the keys in her hand. Even saying Jan's name hit her hard, like the word itself had taste and texture.

Peter cleared his throat. "Um, I know the two of you are…well, I don't know exactly, but…" He hesitated and started over. "I'm taking Chloe back to the Peacock Room Saturday night. I'd like it if you and Jan could meet us there around seven."

"Oh, gee, thanks, but I don't think it's a good idea," Tina said. She wasn't sure how much Peter really knew about her aborted relationship with Jan, but with his sense of decorum he had to recognize her discomfort.

He took her hand in both of his. "I get it," he said. "But if it hadn't been for the two of you, we'd never have met. I hope it's going to be a special night, and it would mean a lot to me if you were there."

Tina didn't want to remind him that the only reason he and Chloe had been invited on the original date was because she and Jan hadn't wanted to be alone together. Only fitting, they had come full circle and *still* didn't want to be around each other. But she heard the meaning behind his invitation.

"Sure. We'll be there. I have to deliver a project I did for her, so I'll ask then." She smiled and punched him lightly on the arm. "I'm guessing we're keeping this a secret from Chloe."

He grinned back, and she knew he was blushing even though it was too dark to see. "I'd prefer it to be a surprise."

Tina opened her car door and climbed in. "She won't hear a word from me. Good night, Peter. And happy birthday."

Chapter Sixteen

Jan opened the door and found Tina on her porch. Damn. Just one glimpse of her, and Jan's fantasies intruded on reality again. Night after night, Jan had imagined Tina coming by, pushing the door open and taking Jan in her arms, leading her upstairs and taking her to bed. Unfortunately, the live version of Tina, propped casually against the porch railing, didn't seem inclined to act out any of Jan's imagined scenarios.

"Hi," Jan said. Not exactly the stuff of passionate fantasies. But it was as much as she could manage. She wasn't sure how to talk to Tina in the light of day. She wanted her still—more than ever—but she refused to even consider a relationship with her beyond their one night together. She had made the right decision, hadn't she? If so, then why couldn't she forget about her and move on?

"Hi yourself," Tina said with a smile. She looked tired, but so did Jan. At least, everyone she knew kept telling her so.

"No, I can't stay," Tina said when Jan tried to wave her inside. Jan stepped onto the porch and pulled the door shut behind her, leaning back against it. "I just came by to give you this," Tina continued, handing Jan a small folder. "It's your dad's video."

"Oh, thank you," Jan said, curious to see the finished product, even though it meant Tina was one step closer to leaving Spokane for good. All for the best. Maybe once she was across the Cascades, Jan could forget about her. Still, she couldn't stop her perverse attempts to make Tina stay. "Don't you want to watch it with us? I mean, because Dad would want you to."

"I think it's something just the two of you should share," Tina said. "Because it's a father-daughter thing, not because I don't want to be around him. Or you."

"I'll…I'll let you know how he likes it," Jan said.

"Tomorrow night?" Tina asked.

"Sure, I guess I can call you then," Jan said, confused by the request.

Tina shook her head. "Peter wants us to meet him and Chloe for a drink at the Peacock Room tomorrow night. I tried to get us out of it, but it's supposed to be sort of a special night. And a secret one, so don't mention it to Chloe."

"The same Chloe who's been reading bridal magazines all week?" Jan asked. Tina laughed and Jan joined in. She had missed the sound of Tina's laughter. "Well, she won't hear about it from me."

"We'll let poor Peter think he's fooled us all," Tina said. "So, about seven? I'll see you there?"

"Sure, I suppose. Although I'm surprised you'd even want to be in the same room as a marriage proposal. Aren't you afraid some of that commitment might rub off?"

"Actually, no," Tina said with a shrug. "He seems happy. And, you know, my reluctance to be in a committed relationship is no different from you saying you'll find one at some unspecified future date. We're both afraid of the same thing. You might have set a pretend date for your chance at love, but you're every bit as determined to avoid it as I've been."

Tina turned and walked down the steps. Jan could only stare after her, her mouth open but no words of rebuttal expressed. Ridiculous. Of course she wasn't afraid of finding someone and settling down. It's what she'd always dreamed of. As soon as she had her home and life with her dad in order. And as soon as she could be certain nothing would change and no one would leave and hurt her ever again. Admittedly, her dream didn't seem to match reality—with its alarming lack of guarantees—but it was a safe dream to have.

Tina paused halfway down the walk and turned to face Jan again. "Oh, by the way," she said, "tomorrow night will give us a chance to talk about your dad's apartment, too. If he's going to be staying here with you, I wouldn't mind subletting long term. My Uncle Nick has some potential jobs lined up for me, and I thought I might stay in Spokane a little longer."

She left without waiting for an answer. Jan held the DVD folder against her chest as she watched Tina drive away. She sighed and went into the house. Right now, she needed to spend some time reliving the past. Because the future suddenly seemed gloriously terrifying, and much closer than she had anticipated.

❖

"I smell popcorn," Glen said as he came into the kitchen.

"I have a video for us to watch. Tina made it," Jan added. She handed her dad a can of Coke and carried her drink and the popcorn out to the living room.

"Isn't she here to watch it with us?" he asked.

"She couldn't stay," Jan said, avoiding his eyes. Jan knew he was aware of her jumbled feelings about Tina, even though he had carefully avoided mentioning her until now. He was giving her time to work through her problems and being as quietly supportive as he always had been. She had eaten so many blueberry pancakes in the past week, she worried she might turn purple.

Once they were settled on the couch, Jan started the movie. She had the odd, disconnected feeling of watching the actual film while simultaneously imagining Tina editing it. She loved the thought of Tina thinking and planning and creating, the intense look on her face when she was wrestling an idea into the shape she wanted. The opening shot was a video clip of an F-15 performing a midair refueling behind a KC-135. The United States Air Force song played in the background. Jan knew this wasn't her dad's footage. Tina had done the research and found the right planes, the right song, to grab the attention of her audience. Jan felt her eyes well up a little at the guilty thought of her dad giving up his chance to fly the plane he really loved. Just for her. But when she glanced over at him, he was smiling without a trace of sadness.

"What a sight, isn't it? I can't believe Tina did this, the same woman who thought that one airplane taking off at Felts was four different ones," he said with a laugh, reaching for a handful of popcorn. "She's amazing. I mean, only if you think so, too," he added with a fatherly pat on her knee. "You know where my loyalties lie."

Jan laughed. "She *is* something special," she said. She took a drink of her pop and watched a montage of her dad moving through the ranks in his military career. She recognized some of the marches and some themes from war movies on Tina's soundtrack, most of them from her dad's collection. Tina had added some of her own selections as well, and the theme of the music matched the emotions in the photos perfectly.

After the initial career section, the rest of the DVD consisted of photos of Jan and her dad, or Jan alone. Tina had arranged them thematically, and Jan watched as a series of birthday parties, then school science projects, then pink bedrooms unfolded on the screen. The background music reflected the changes in setting, varying to represent different states and countries, but Tina had captured the constancy of the images themselves.

When the video ended, Jan and her dad sat in silence, their Cokes warm and most of the popcorn uneaten. Jan felt vulnerable, exposed, grateful, *seen*. Tina had captured her essence, the core elements of her life that remained consistent, even though the settings changed. School, learning, animals, exploration, art.

"It was supposed to be all about your life," Jan said finally, embarrassed to have been the center of the movie, to have been understood so deeply by Tina.

"It was," Glen said, putting his arm around her shoulders. "Tina got it exactly right."

"She did, didn't she," Jan agreed softly. She turned and buried her face in her dad's shoulder.

She felt him sigh. "Such beautiful memories." He paused and continued in a quiet voice. "I don't want to lose them."

And I don't want to lose you. But she couldn't say it out loud. "I know," she said instead.

Only when he hugged her tighter did she realize she was crying. Tina's sequential themes kept playing through Jan's mind. She had spent her life focused on the things she lacked—one house, one city, one set of friends. She hadn't really started to appreciate the richness of all she did have until she was threatened with its loss. But Tina had done more than simply show Jan a new way to look at her life—she had become a part of that life. Jan had been holding on to a cookie-cutter vision of the perfect home, family, and love, but Tina had shown her how much more vivid and wonderful the real thing could be. Messy and unpredictable. Passionate and loving. Filled with laughter and set to music.

Her dad gave her shoulder a pat. "Well, there's no room for fear in the future," he said in his normal voice. "We can spend the summer making new memories and get Tina to make a brand-new DVD next year."

Jan smiled and dried her eyes. Definitely a yes to the memories. And a maybe to Tina's involvement in the future. Still, she had seen Jan more clearly than anyone ever had, and she seemed determined to stick around. Jan had no idea what might happen next week, next month, next year, and she had to accept that her well-ordered plans didn't seem to apply to her new life. She might just have to learn to play it by ear.

❖

Jan came around the corner from the lobby and saw Tina. She was waiting outside the bar, near a glass door leading to the street. Waiting for her. Jan hesitated on the short staircase, just wanting some time to look at Tina, unobserved. She was wearing a green silk blouse, open at the neck, and her hair was loose and glowing in the waning light of day. So beautiful. And so cautious-looking. Hands in the pockets of her dark slacks, body held too stiffly. Jan sighed in relief. She didn't want Tina to be uncomfortable—and she hoped she wouldn't be for long—but she was glad to know tonight mattered to Tina. To both of them. She came down the last of the stairs and walked over to Tina.

"Hi," she said. Tina turned quickly and faced her.

"Hi. I thought you'd come in this way, but you must have parked on the other side…" Her voice faded to a stop.

"I used the valet," Jan admitted. "It's so hard to find a good place to park this time of night."

"I know," Tina said. "I had to walk four blocks." She paused and gave Jan a small grin. "Nice weather, though."

Jan couldn't control her answering smile. "A little cool, but I'm hoping it will warm up this evening."

Tina laughed, looking more like her regular self. "Me, too. In fact, it already feels more comfortable. Shall we join the sappy lovebirds?"

"I suppose we have to," Jan said. She headed toward the door of the bar, but Tina stopped her with a hand on her arm. She withdrew it before Jan had time to enjoy the fleeting contact.

"I wanted to ask about the video. Was it all right?"

Jan heard the hesitation in Tina's voice. The uncertainty. She wanted to reassure her, but her eyes filled with tears at the thought of watching the DVD with her dad. She would never again take for granted any time they spent together, and watching the DVD Tina had made was a memory she'd cherish forever. She wasn't in control enough to explain to Tina what a gift she'd given them, but she hoped Tina would understand. She looked away and blinked, trying to regain her composure. "It was perfect," she managed.

The ice melted completely as Tina came forward and wrapped her arms around Jan in a quick hug. "I'm so glad," she said, stepping back. "But we can talk about it another time."

Jan nodded and opened the door. "After you," she said.

Tina hesitated in the doorway, and Jan almost bumped into her back "Are you going to shut this behind me and leave?"

"Not a chance," Jan said, close enough to smell the hint of rosin in Tina's hair. She would bet anything Tina had been playing the fiddle right before she came.

Chloe and Peter were tucked in a corner of the bar, wrapped in their own private world, but they stood up as soon as Jan and Tina got to the table.

"We're engaged," Chloe said, nearly bouncing as she showed off her ring.

Tina clutched her chest and staggered back a step. "This is such unexpected and shocking news," she said. She pulled out chairs for herself and for Jan. "I need to sit down before I faint. Jan, did you have any idea?"

"I certainly did not," Jan said as she sat next to Tina. "I think I need a cold cloth for my forehead."

"And I need a drink to soothe my startled nerves," Tina said, snapping her fingers at Peter.

"Oh, that sounds better," Jan agreed. "Me, too."

Peter rolled his eyes at Chloe. "Tina was annoying as a child. We thought she'd grow out of it, but apparently she hasn't. I'll go order us some champagne."

Chloe gave him a kiss before he left the table, and then she sat down again, glaring at Jan and Tina. "The two of you need to stick together. No one else thinks you're funny."

Jan looked around the crowded room. "How'd he ask? Did he get down on one knee in front of all these strangers?"

Tina snorted with laughter. "Are you kidding? Peter? Of course he did. He couldn't stray off the traditional path if you gave him a hard shove."

"It was very romantic," Chloe said with a frown.

"I'm sure it was, and really, we want to hear all about it," Jan said. She kicked Tina hard in the shin when she seemed about to protest.

"Ow. Yes, please. I apparently need to hear every detail."

Jan listened, biting her lip to keep from laughing out loud, as Chloe told them the story of Peter's very conventional down-on-one-knee proposal. She wasn't even sure why she found it so funny. Maybe because Tina had been so right about him. Or because she was so relieved to be on comfortable joking terms with Tina again. One more piece falling into place. Sex and laughter, shared thoughts and mutual comfort. The shape of her relationship with Tina had more depth and dimension than Jan had ever known.

Peter returned, followed closely by a waiter carrying a bottle of chilled champagne. He popped the cork and carefully filled four glasses with gold liquid.

Tina lifted her glass, watching the light reflect off the small bubbles suspended in the wine. The color of Jan's hair, sifting through Tina's fingers, brushing softly against her face. More intoxicating than the liquor. Tina glanced over at her. She was smiling tonight. Happy and more relaxed than Tina had ever seen her. She wondered what had caused the transformation.

"I'd like to propose a toast." Peter's voice broke into her thoughts. "To the women who brought me and Chloe together, earning our undying gratitude. Tina and Jan."

Tina was about to take a drink, but he continued with his toast. "Who also are, incidentally, the only ones who haven't said we're crazy to be so sure of our future together even though we've only known each other a few weeks. It's as if they somehow understand firsthand how two people can fall in love so quickly. Cheers."

Chloe winked at him as they clinked glasses and drank. Jan took a sip, too, but she set her glass down quickly. Tina glared at her cousin, but he only smiled in return as if daring her to make a scene. She bit back any sarcastic retorts and downed half of her champagne in one swallow.

Tina partially listened to Chloe's detailed plans for the wedding, but most of her attention was focused on Jan. She had been apprehensive about coming tonight, unsure how they would get along, but they seemed to have returned to a friendly rapport. She had been hoping for at least this much. She enjoyed Jan's company, loved the way they communicated and laughed and inspired each other. For a moment, earlier, she had even considered staying longer in Spokane so they'd have time to develop a deeper friendship. But sitting here now, so close she only had to shift her leg to be in contact with Jan's thigh, she had to face the truth. She was learning to make compromises in her family relationships, to accept faults and try to find a truce, a way to move forward in peace. But she couldn't do the same thing with Jan. Because she loved her, she couldn't just be friends with her. It was all or nothing. Love. Or Tina had to walk away.

"It's amazing how you managed to come up with all these ideas for your wedding after only being engaged for fifteen minutes," Tina commented when Chloe took a break from talking to give Peter another embarrassing kiss. Jan covered her mouth as if to hide her laughter, but she didn't do a very good job of it. Tina smiled in her direction. She was glad the two of them could have a fun night together. So there'd be no hard feelings between them when she left.

The night ended as soon as the bottle was empty. Chloe and Peter were off to share their good news with two sets of parents, and Tina stayed behind to settle the bill she insisted on paying. Jan lingered beside her.

Tina signed the credit card slip and stood up. She wondered what the protocol was in this situation. Did she shake Jan's hand? Give her a hug? Just drift off into the night?

Jan settled the dilemma, at least for the moment. "Stay and have one more drink with me?" she asked.

Tina could only say yes.

CHAPTER SEVENTEEN

Tina watched as Jan drew patterns in the condensation on her glass, a nervous habit she had noticed a couple of times before. She wondered what Jan wanted to talk about, why she had asked Tina to stay. The laughing, relaxed Jan from earlier in the bar had disappeared, leaving a much more serious Jan in her place.

"Dad really loved the DVD," she finally said. "The opening scene was great, with the refueling tanker and the air force music."

Tina shrugged. "It's what I do."

"It was very professional. The editing was smooth, and the way you connected the music with the pictures…well, I knew you'd be good at that after seeing the websites you've created. Especially the ones related to music. I'm sure Dad will watch it over and over. It's so much better than just shuffling through pictures."

"Good," Tina said, sensing her own growing reticence as Jan seemed to become more nervous and chatty.

"I'm glad you didn't stay while we played it the first time," Jan admitted, staring at her glass and wiping off her sketches as if she were erasing a chalkboard.

"Oh?" Tina asked, trying unsuccessfully to keep the surprise out of her voice.

"It was…" Jan shrugged and met Tina's gaze. "It was very emotional. Because they're Dad's memories, but also because of how you exposed what my life was really like."

"And how did I do that?" Tina asked, more gently this time.

"You showed me how much I had. How much love and stability and support." Jan turned to look out the window, and Tina gave in to her desire to touch her. Just a simple touch as she reached for Jan's hand. "I had been looking at the superficial things I was missing," Jan continued, wrapping her fingers around Tina's. "A house and a yard and a dog. They might have been nice to have, but only if I had been living there with my dad. On their own, they wouldn't have made me any happier than I was. I guess I had given them too much power in my mind, as if a bunch of wood or bricks or grass was magically going to make me feel at home."

"Instead, you had pink paint and airplane rides and trips to the zoo," Tina said.

"And you helped me see how much those things meant," Jan said with a sad-looking smile. "You saw deeper than I did. And I did the same thing with you."

"What do you mean?" Tina asked, desperately trying to follow Jan's train of thought. She knew the conversation was important, and she had to pay attention, but it was growing increasingly difficult while Jan was rubbing her thumb slowly back and forth along the palm of Tina's hand. She had taken Jan's hand in a gesture of support, but the contact was quickly growing more suggestive. With Jan doing the initiating. A feeling of hope stirred in Tina, matching her growing arousal in intensity.

"I saw your surface and thought you were sexy. Someone good for a one-night stand. I heard about your reputation and didn't believe you'd ever be someone I could trust so much."

Tina laughed. "Well, I didn't help by doing my best to live down to those expectations. I didn't realize there was more to me than fleeting relationships and no-strings sex, either. Until you. Until you made me require more from myself. Because I wanted to give you more."

Jan disengaged her hand when the waiter brought their bill. Tina reached for her wallet, but Jan stopped her. "This one's on me," she said, signing her name on the slip of paper. "I'll just charge it to my room."

Tina kept silent until they were alone again. "Your room?" she asked in a casual voice. At least she meant it to be casual, but the pitch sounded higher than normal. She hadn't been sure where they were headed, but now she knew. Once again, the line between fantasy and reality became blurred. And suddenly reality had the potential to be everything she'd dreamed it might be. "You're staying here?"

Jan shrugged, looking about as casual as Tina sounded. "I needed a little break, so I thought a night in a fancy hotel would be fun."

"You made a good choice," Tina said. She put her hand under the table and gently brushed against Jan's thigh. "The pillow-topped mattresses are so comfortable."

Jan cleared her throat. "And roomy," she said.

Tina felt a funny sense of being wrenched back in time. But to a time that had never existed. The night Jan had wanted to call her, invite her for a drink in an anonymous hotel bar, lead her upstairs. Tina wanted to take everything she knew Jan was offering. Gratitude for the video and for Tina's honest representation of Jan's past. A chance to live out yet another fantasy. Time for just the two of them, in this place on the edge of reality. If their previous night together was any indication of how this one would go, Tina knew she didn't have any choice but to say yes. She raked her fingernails along the outer seam of Jan's slacks.

"And did you see the shower stall?" Tina asked, curving her hand over Jan's leg and tugging until Jan separated her thighs enough for Tina to press her knee between them. She pictured Jan pressed against the marble walls of the shower. Wet. Hot. "It's huge, and the spray is very...powerful."

"I know," Jan said. "I took a shower before I came down here."

"Thinking of me?" Tina asked. Jan had started to draw on her glass again, and Tina captured her hand, rubbing her thumb over the wetness on Jan's fingertips.

"Yes," Jan said in a barely audible voice. "Very lonely. And thinking of you."

Tina raised Jan's hand and lightly brushed a kiss over the backs of her fingers. "I can take care of the lonely part."

"You're quite good at this," Jan said, ending with a little gasp as Tina pushed harder with her knee.

"I suppose the snappy comeback is *lots of practice, baby,* but it's not true," Tina said, letting go of Jan's hand and reaching up to brush Jan's bangs out of her eyes. She wondered if she should act cooler, less affected by their little performance. She didn't want to spoil Jan's fantasy, but she had to be honest. "This is all new to me," she admitted. "We're sitting here fully dressed, but I've never felt so naked with another woman."

"I understand," Jan said. "I feel more exposed, but safer and more protected, than I've ever felt before." She cleared her throat again, taking one last swallow of her drink. "My room also has a magnificent view of downtown," she said. "Do you want to see it?"

Tina answered by getting to her feet and reaching for Jan's hand. She tugged her toward the elevators and pressed the button.

"You helped me, too, you know," she said, watching the floor numbers light up while they waited for the elevator, avoiding Jan's eyes. "When you yelled at me that morning." Tina held up a hand to keep Jan from interrupting when she looked ready to protest. "I thought I was free, independent, but you made me realize I was connected to my family. By my resentment, the hurt I kept with me from when I was a kid. But connected in some good ways, too, like my relationship with Peter and the memories I share with my aunt and uncle."

Tina shook her head. "I always claimed I'd never be tied down, never be caught by anyone or anything, but I was wrong. I'm so tangled up with my music, my friends, my family, I can't imagine my life without them." *Or you*, she wanted to add. Her connection to Jan was growing stronger all the time. Making it so easy to joke with her, to talk to her, to excite her, to be aroused by her, but at the same time, so difficult to share the real truth. To say *I love you*. Jan wanted tonight, wanted one more fantasy, but Tina desired much more.

Jan stepped on the elevator when it arrived. "A lot of people care about you, Tina," she said as she inserted her room key card and pushed the floor number. "I'm glad I could—"

Tina grabbed Jan's elbow, spinning her around and pressing her against the wall the second the door slid closed. She was rough enough to startle a squeak of surprise from Jan, but not enough to hurt her. She noticed Jan's immediate response—her darkening eyes, flushed chest, and hitched breathing—right before she lowered her mouth to Jan's. After the coy dance in the bar, Tina wanted to take her, to claim her, to leave no room for doubt in Jan's mind about how much Tina needed her.

Unfortunately, she managed to convince herself as well. The chime of the elevator as it reached their floor startled them apart, as if it signaled the end of a prizefighting round. They stood, inches apart, staring at each other, and only the quick slap of Tina's hand kept the elevator doors from closing again, with them still inside. She stepped off the elevator with Jan, but she couldn't make herself walk down the hall.

"I can't do it," she said when Jan turned to look at her, a confused expression on her face. She had thought she could. Sacrifice her tentative dream of forever for this one perfect night. Walk away in the morning, certain beyond question that her future would hold nothing but the memory of love.

"I don't understand," Jan said finally. "What am I supposed to do?"

Tina shook her head, frustrated. "This isn't part of the game, Jan. I want you, and I'd like nothing better than to lock you in that hotel room and act out every fantasy you can imagine. But I can't."

"Why not?"

Tina struggled with the truth. She had made a decision, and she knew she had to stick to it. "Because I love you. It's all or nothing, Jan. Not one night, or one weekend. Forever, or I have to walk away right now."

"I don't want you to go," Jan said, the same struggle written clearly on her face as she started to cry. "But I can't ask you to stay with me…"

Tina closed the gap between them and tenderly cupped Jan's chin. She kissed her, long and slow and deep. "Ask me to stay," she said, her voice raspy with desire.

Jan shook her head. "I have nothing to offer, no idea what the future will bring. I can't ask you to—"

Tina broke away. The first wrenching step was the hardest, and she had to fight against her body's urge to stay, anyway. But she refused to settle now. She knew what she wanted, and she wouldn't accept less. She turned her back on Jan and jabbed at the elevator's down button.

Jan stared at Tina's stiffly held spine, her tightly crossed arms. Nothing to offer. She repeated the words in her mind. Nothing but a sick father, an uncertain path ahead, debt, boring life in a small city. Love.

"Stay," she said. She cleared her throat and spoke louder. "Please, stay. I love you, too."

The words were barely out of her mouth before Tina was on her, holding her, kissing her, shoving her back until they collided with the wall. Jan laughed through her tears.

"We have a room, you know," she said, arching away from the wall as Tina kissed her jawline, below her ear.

"A room, yes," Tina said with a laugh. "Sounds good."

She took Jan's hand and started down the hall, looking back over her shoulder when Jan resisted.

"No second thoughts," she said, a touch of pleading in her voice.

"Never. But the room is this way." Jan pointed behind her. She headed in the right direction, Tina close at her heels. Time and again, Jan had imagined this walk down the hall to a hotel room, to a night of sex, to a night with Tina. But she had never dreamed the words *I love you*, much less the full emotions behind them, would have played any part in the scene. She had expected to feel this breathless because of excitement, arousal, passion. Not because she was so deeply in awe of the love Tina offered.

Jan barely had time to pull her key card out of the lock before Tina had her inside, the door shut and Jan pressed against it. Tina kissed her hard, not breaking contact while she unbuttoned Jan's shirt and yanked it off her shoulders. Jan struggled to get enough air as she kicked off her shoes and fumbled with the buttons on Tina's shirt.

Jan had expected Tina to turn slow and gentle once they were alone. Gazing into each other's eyes after their declaration of love, not hungrily tearing off clothes as quickly as possible. She had no complaints, and she matched Tina kiss for kiss as they struggled toward the bed, until the emotions behind Tina's feverish ardor finally penetrated her brain. Desperation. The fear of losing something so important she felt incapable of existing without it. Jan knew the feeling well, but she hadn't realized Tina had been experiencing it, too.

She pulled back, stiffening her arms to keep Tina away. "You really didn't think I felt the same way, did you?" she asked softly.

Tina shook her head, the vulnerability in her eyes enough to make Jan want to cry again.

"Tell me again," Tina said, pushing Jan so she sat down on the edge of the bed.

"I love you," Jan said as Tina hooked her fingers in Jan's underwear and slid it off.

"Again," Tina said, pressing on Jan's thighs.

Jan spread her legs, and Tina knelt between them. "I love you," she said, laughing a bit nervously at the hungry look on Tina's face.

"Again," Tina said, with a decidedly predatory smile, before she lowered her head and took Jan in her mouth.

Jan couldn't say the words, but she knew Tina heard them in Jan's sharp, climactic cry.

❖

"What's this?" Tina asked as she came out of the bathroom holding two empty wrappers. The sight of Jan nestling her obviously very relaxed body under the covers almost sidetracked her. Almost.

"Garbage?" Jan suggested.

"You ate *both* packets of peanut brittle?" Tina remembered the candy left by housekeeping on her dresser every night when she had stayed here, only weeks ago, although it seemed like a lifetime away.

"I was here all afternoon," Jan said. "And I was nervous. I would've emptied the minibar if the room had one."

"You know I have a sweet tooth," Tina said, trying to sound menacing. She wasn't doing a good job of it, distracted as she was by Jan's naked body. And by the way she was patting the empty space in the bed invitingly. She felt a corresponding tug on her body with every move Jan made. Connected. In a way she'd never felt before.

"I think they sell boxes of it in the hotel lobby."

"I don't feel like walking that far," Tina complained, tossing the wrappers aside and climbing onto the bed. She straddled Jan, one hand braced on either side of her head. "Gumdrop," she added.

Jan grabbed her wrists and flipped both of them over, nearly fast enough to knock the wind out of Tina. "We have *got* to do something about those pet names of yours," Jan said. She kept Tina's wrists firmly anchored to the bed as she lowered her mouth and wrapped her lips around one of Tina's erect nipples.

Tina struggled against her hold just a little. Not hard enough to break free. "Aw, Pookie Bear, you know you love it…Ouch! You bit me," Tina said, as surprised by Jan's teeth as she was by her unrepentant smile.

"I'd be concerned about your comfort if you weren't laughing so hard," Jan said as she turned her attention to Tina's other nipple, using only her tongue this time. She let go of Tina's wrists and dropped to her elbows, resting some of her weight on Tina as she slid her hand down Tina's waist.

Tina tried to make up more names, but her brain was giving up the fight. All she knew was Jan. Jan's hands and lips moved over her, making her flesh vibrate and sing at every point of contact. Ceding all control to her body, she arched her back and was rewarded when Jan sucked harder on her breast.

"Feels…so good, love muffin," she said with a gasp, twisting away when Jan pinched her hip roughly, only to push toward her hand again in an irresistible desire for contact.

She felt Jan shift to one side, and then her fingers were stroking Tina, entering her smoothly. Tina cried out, unable to keep still as Jan's palm pressed against her clit. "Oh, yes…baby, yes," Tina cried as she came, throwing her head back against the pillow, offering everything she had to Jan.

When Tina lay quietly, trying to control her breathing, Jan slid up the bed, resting her head on Tina's chest. "I called you baby and you let me come," Tina said, unable to keep from grinning as she rubbed her thumb over Jan's dove tattoo. "Does that mean we've found your pet name?"

"Definitely not," Jan murmured against Tina's breast. Worn out as she was, Tina still responded immediately to the caress of breath and lips. Brought to life by Jan's touch. Sexually and emotionally. Heart and soul. "I was simply obeying a mindless and primal urge to take you. You'll pay for the name later."

Tina smiled, her lips pressing against Jan's hair. She couldn't wait.

Chapter Eighteen

Six months later, Tina walked up the steps to the church altar and stood quietly, off to one side and flanked by mammoth arrangements of white lilies and roses, until the church fell silent. She lifted her acoustic instrument and settled it under her chin, immediately sensing the connection she felt with her father every time she played his violin. Her electric fiddle would have sounded great in the church, with its vaulted ceilings and deep alcoves, but her dad belonged here today. She tapped a rhythm with her foot before drawing her bow over the strings in the first notes of the Irish jig "Haste to the Wedding." Later in the ceremony, she would play more serious and traditional songs, with her quartet and alone, but Peter and Chloe had chosen this lively tune as the perfect beginning for their wedding celebration.

Tina needed to play through the short song several times while the families were seated and the wedding party came down the aisle, so she'd add some ornamentation and variety to keep the music interesting. Last night, she had sat down with a paper and pen, ready to organize her thoughts and plan how to vary the tune. She knew Andy would have been proud of her intentions, but less than impressed with her results. Tina had left the paper blank, choosing instead to improvise during the ceremony. Partly because she truly believed the music would be a better gift to Peter if it was heartfelt and spontaneous. And mostly because Jan had been kissing the back of her neck in the most enjoyable way. Tina had opted to throw her pen aside and let preparation be damned. Any time she had to choose between her lover and another task, Jan *always* won. And she always would.

Tina let her violin sing with quiet simplicity the first time through the jig. The sound resonated through the finely varnished wood and filled the church with its joyous rhythm as Peter and the minister came through a side door and stood in front of the altar. Tina smiled at her cousin, awed by the expression on his face as he waited there for Chloe. She blinked back tears as she realized how much his happiness meant to her and how close she had come to shutting him out of her life forever. Over the past months, they had grown closer, bound by family ties and by music and by a simple fondness for each other's company. She and Jan spent several evenings a week with Peter and Chloe, no longer needing them as buffers or bodyguards but simply as friends.

The two families were seated while Tina repeated the tune. The sight of her grandmother stirred those old resentments to life—and maybe always would—but Tina was learning to deal with her anger over the past. Jan helped, listening and always steadfastly taking Tina's side, but injecting reason here and there. And Tina had never realized how much a mere touch—a hand on her knee or a brush of Jan's shoulder—would calm her when Francine pushed her buttons. Simple touch, but the emotion and love ran deep enough to soothe.

The percussive finger rolls and staccato bowing inspired by her grandmother colored the second iteration of the song. She slid through her chords, moving from a minor seventh to a major. Creating a slight dissonance before resolving the tone. She came to the end of the darker, more shaded variation as her aunt and uncle were seated. Uncle Nick winked at her, doing a few steps of a jig before he sat down. Tina laughed along with the rest of the congregation, feeling the tightening in her stomach ease. The nuances of the music had affected her more than she expected, and she felt tears sting her eyes again, mingling with her laughter, as she recalled her uncle's reverent expression when he'd held his late brother's violin before the ceremony.

Tina nearly dropped the precious instrument when she saw Jan start down the aisle. Wearing a silky pearl-gray dress, her blond hair held off her elegant neck with a pearl clip, and a bouquet of lilies dripping from her arms, she was gorgeous. Tina pulled herself together and played the third version of the song for Jan. Legato bowing, bending and sliding the blue notes into chord resolutions. She let her fiddle sing of love in an almost human voice, slowing the tempo of the jig and creating her own combination of Celtic music and blues. Jan waved subtly at her dad before turning her attention back to Tina. Jan, loving her and being loved by her every day and night. Meals with her and Glen, quiet talks and bursts of laughter, family and home. Tina's entire life was walking up the aisle toward her. To stand by Chloe today, but on another day? Maybe she'd be walking to meet Tina at the altar.

Jan took her place as Tina finished the bluesy variation. One more time through, as Chloe came up the aisle. Tina glanced at her quartet. David had been tapping his fingers on the body of his cello and his feet on the floor, as if unable to resist the tune's infectious rhythm. Andy had sat through the music with her arm draped over her viola, her fingers twitching over the strings as if she was longing to play. Even Richard had been rocking back and forth along with the song. Tina had planned to play the entire piece as a solo, but she changed her mind when she saw Chloe standing in the back of the church with her parents. Tina gave her quartet a short nod, and they moved their instruments into playing position as if on cue, joining her in the final variation of the tune.

Reading her with unerring accuracy, Richard took over the melody while David and Andy added depth to the music with their harmony. Tina let her violin sing as she played the high, joyful notes of the descant. She had planned to spend her life alone, keeping friends, lovers, and family at a distance. But everything was different now. Connections. Tina looked only at Jan as she finished the processional music. A love she had never expected. A love she couldn't live without. Tina had been stuck playing the same song over and over. *Leave me alone. Don't get too close.* As Tina lowered her violin, Jan gave her a smile full of love and promise. Jan had made Tina change her tune, adapting and improvising. And the possibilities of this new music were limitless.

About the Author

Karis Walsh is a horseback riding instructor who lives on a small farm in the Pacific Northwest. When she isn't teaching or writing, she enjoys spending time outside with her animals, reading, playing the viola, and riding with friends.

Books Available from Bold Strokes Books

Battle Axe by Carsen Taite. How close is too close? Bounty hunter Luca Bennett will soon find out. (978-1-60282-871-1)

Improvisation by Karis Walsh. High school geometry teacher Jan Carroll thinks she's figured out the shape of her life and her future, until graphic artist and fiddle player Tina Nelson comes along and teaches her to improvise. (978-1-60282-872-8)

For Want of a Fiend by Barbara Ann Wright. Without her Fiendish power, can Princess Katya and her consort Starbride stop a magic-wielding madman from sparking an uprising in the kingdom of Farraday? (978-1-60282-873-5)

Broken in Soft Places by Fiona Zedde. The instant Sara Chambers meets the seductive and sinful Merille Thompson, she falls hard, but knowing the difference between love and a dangerous, all-consuming desire is just one of the lessons Sara must learn before it's too late. (978-1-60282-876-6)

Healing Hearts by Donna K. Ford. Running from tragedy, the women of Willow Springs find that with friendship, there is hope, and with love, there is everything. (978-1-60282-877-3)

Desolation Point by Cari Hunter. When a storm strands Sarah Kent in the North Cascades, Alex Pascal is determined to find her. Neither imagines the dangers they will face when a ruthless criminal begins to hunt them down. (978-1-60282-865-0)

I Remember by Julie Cannon. What happens when you can never forget the first kiss, the first touch, the first taste of lips on skin? What happens when you know you will remember every single detail of a mysterious woman? (978-1-60282-866-7)

The Gemini Deception by Kim Baldwin and Xenia Alexiou. The truth, the whole truth, and nothing but lies. Book six in the Elite Operatives series. (978-1-60282-867-4)

Scarlet Revenge by Sheri Lewis Wohl. When faith alone isn't enough, will the love of one woman be strong enough to save a vampire from damnation? (978-1-60282-868-1)

Ghost Trio by Lillian Q. Irwin. When Lee Howe hears the voice of her dead lover singing to her, is it a hallucination, a ghost, or something more sinister? (978-1-60282-869-8)

The Princess Affair by Nell Stark. Rhodes Scholar Kerry Donovan arrives at Oxford ready to focus on her studies, but her life and her priorities are thrown into chaos when she catches the eye of Her Royal Highness Princess Sasha. (978-1-60282-858-2)

The Chase by Jesse J. Thoma. When Isabelle Rochat's life is threatened, she receives the unwelcome protection and attention of bounty hunter Holt Lasher who vows to keep Isabelle safe at all costs. (978-1-60282-859-9)

The Lone Hunt by L.L. Raand. In a world where humans and praeterns conspire for the ultimate power, violence is a way of life… and death. A Midnight Hunters novel. (978-1-60282-860-5)

The Supernatural Detective by Crin Claxton. Tony Carson sees dead people. With a drag queen for a spirit guide and a devastatingly attractive herbalist for a client, she's about to discover the spirit world can be a very dangerous world indeed. (978-1-60282-861-2)

Beloved Gomorrah by Justine Saracen. Undersea artists creating their own City on the Plain uncover the truth about Sodom and Gomorrah, whose "one righteous man" is a murderer, rapist, and conspirator in genocide. (978-1-60282-862-9)

Cut to the Chase by Lisa Girolami. Careful and methodical author Paige Cornish falls for brash and wild Hollywood actress Avalon Randolph, but can these opposites find a happy middle ground in a town that never lives in the middle? (978-1-60282-783-7)

More Than Friends by Erin Dutton. Evelyn Fisher thinks she has the perfect role model for a long-term relationship, until her best friends, Kendall and Melanie, split up and all three women must reevaluate their lives and their relationships. (978-1-60282-784-4)

Every Second Counts by D. Jackson Leigh. Every second counts in Bridgette LeRoy's desperate mission to protect her heart and stop Marc Ryder's suicidal return to riding rodeo bulls. (978-1-60282-785-1)

Dirty Money by Ashley Bartlett. Vivian Cooper and Reese DiGiovanni just found out that falling in love is hard. It's even harder when you're running for your life. (978-1-60282-786-8)

Sea Glass Inn by Karis Walsh. When Melinda Andrews commissions a series of mosaics by Pamela Whitford for her new inn, she doesn't expect to be more captivated by the artist than by the paintings. (978-1-60282-771-4)

The Awakening: A Sisters of Spirits novel by Yvonne Heidt. Sunny Skye has interacted with spirits her entire life, but when she runs into Officer Jordan Lawson during a ghost investigation, she discovers more than just facts in a missing girl's cold case file. (978-1-60282-772-1)

Murphy's Law by Yolanda Wallace. No matter how high you climb, you can't escape your past. (978-1-60282-773-8)

Blacker Than Blue by Rebekah Weatherspoon. Threatened with losing her first love to a powerful demon, vampire Cleo Jones is willing to break the ultimate law of the undead to rebuild the family she has lost. (978-1-60282-774-5)

Silver Collar by Gill McKnight. Werewolf Luc Garoul is outlawed and out of control, but can her family track her down before a sinister predator gets there first? Fourth in the Garoul series. (978-1-60282-764-6)

The Dragon Tree Legacy by Ali Vali. For Aubrey Tarver time hasn't dulled the pain of losing her first love Wiley Gremillion, but she has to set that aside when her choices put her life and her family's lives in real danger. (978-1-60282-765-3)

The Midnight Room by Ronica Black. After a chance encounter with the mysterious and brooding Lillian Gray in the "midnight room" of The Griffin, a local lesbian bar, confident and gorgeous Audrey McCarthy learns that her bad-girl behavior isn't bulletproof. (978-1-60282-766-0)

Dirty Sex by Ashley Bartlett. Vivian Cooper and twins Reese and Ryan DiGiovanni stole a lot of money and the guy they took it from wants it back. Like now. (978-1-60282-767-7)

The Storm by Shelley Thrasher. Rural East Texas. 1918. War-weary Jaq Bergeron and marriage-scarred musician Molly Russell try to salvage love from the devastation of the war abroad and natural disasters at home. (978-1-60282-780-6)

Crossroads by Radclyffe. Dr. Hollis Monroe specializes in short-term relationships but when she meets pregnant mother-to-be Annie Colfax, fate brings them together at a crossroads that will change their lives forever. (978-1-60282-756-1)

Beyond Innocence by Carsen Taite. When a life is on the line, love has to wait. Doesn't it? (978-1-60282-757-8)

Heart Block by Melissa Brayden. Socialite Emory Owen and struggling single mom Sarah Matamoros are perfectly suited for each other but face a difficult time when trying to merge their contrasting worlds and the people in them. If love truly exists, can it find a way? (978-1-60282-758-5)

Pride and Joy by M.L. Rice. Perfect Bryce Montgomery is her parents' pride and joy, but when they discover that their daughter is a lesbian, her world changes forever. (978-1-60282-759-2)

Ladyfish by Andrea Bramhall. Finn's escape to the Florida Keys leads her straight into the arms of scuba diving instructor Oz as she fights for her freedom, their blossoming love…and her life! (978-1-60282-747-9)

Spanish Heart by Rachel Spangler. While on a mission to find herself in Spain, Ren Molson runs the risk of losing her heart to her tour guide, Lina Montero. (978-1-60282-748-6)

boldstrokesbooks.com
Bold Strokes Books
Quality and Diversity in LGBTQ Literature
victory
EDITIONS
Drama
MATINEE BOOKS
SCI-FI
E-BOOKS
MYSTERY
erotica
BSB
SOLILOQUY
EROTICA
YOUNG
ADULT
BOLD
STROKES
BOOKS
LiBERTY
Romance
W·E·B·S·T·O·R·E
PRINT AND EBOOKS